Capitally Matched

RACHEL HOLM

A Note from the Author

While this book is intended to be mostly a low-angst romantic comedy, there are real life emotions and experiences the hero and heroine go through that could be difficult for some readers. These include: Parental coldness/Feelings of failed parental expectations, Death of Parent (off-page, past). I have done my best to treat these with care and hope you will agree, but please take care of yourself first and foremost.

This book contains graphic language, including a few explicit, consensual sex acts between the hero and heroine, though references to sexual thoughts and content occurs throughout the book. I recognize the inclusion of this content may mean this book is not for you (or it may confirm that it very much is).

For anyone who has put their faith in themselves and taken a leap; this one's for you.

CHAPTER

One

HAYDEN

I was sitting on a pile of boxes in the hallway of what had been my home as of four hours ago, sweating in the August heat. As it turns out, if your name isn't on the lease, then it never really was your home. I found myself questioning exactly how my life came to this.

The green door of the apartment to my left cracked open and my girlfriend, well ex-girlfriend, appeared.

"Here. I found your Star Wars bottle opener in the kitchen," Veronica extended her arm out the slim opening, setting Darth Vader on top of a stack of three boxes, piled next to the door frame. "You're going to get all these boxes out of here, right? The neighbors are going to complain when they have to play Ninja Warrior to get to their doors."

I turned my head, certain my disbelief was written all over my features.

"I got here fifteen minutes ago. I need to figure out where I'm going to sleep tonight, let alone how I'm going to get all of this stuff out of here. Your psychic didn't give you any leads on a new apartment for me, did she?"

At this, Veronica swung the door open, her bright red hair

fanning over her shoulder. She leaned on the doorjamb and folded her bare arms with a huff.

"Like I said when you got home, my psychic in Boston has been having serious doubts about our relationship for months, which is why I didn't put your name on the lease. Miss Hindy recommended Madam London as the best psychic in Washington, DC, and suggested I didn't make any final decisions until my energy coalesced in this latitude and longitude. But Madam London's reading today was certain. We have no future. You have no right to this apartment after only seventy-two hours, so figure it out. Goodbye, Hayden."

With that, the door slammed shut with a resolute bang. Of course, the psychic-obsessed paralegal from my brother's Boston office, starting at Georgetown Law next week, would have a firm grasp on DC tenant law, but also make major life decisions by what a complete stranger saw in a crystal ball. Veronica and I hadn't worked for the same department when we started dating late last year; she was a fun distraction from the not-so-subtle hints Duncan had been dropping about it being time for me to take on the CIO job at his firm's US headquarters. Five years working in Boston after college and grad school, and now I was in another big city I was sure I would hate, starting at a job I wasn't even sure I wanted, but I owed a lot to Duncan, so here I was.

I felt my phone vibrate next to me. Speak of the oldest brother.

"Hi, Duncan. How's Brussels?"

"Sproutless. I got your text and only have five minutes before dinner. Veronica kicked you out and is moving to London?"

Looks like some things got a bit jumbled when I was texting under duress. I would need to look back later to see what my text actually said in my SOS message.

"It's a long story, but in short, I need a place to stay and some help to get all my belongings out of a fifth-floor hallway in Georgetown."

I heard rustling on the other line, which I took to mean Duncan had put me on speakerphone and was putting on his tuxedo. Soon, he'd be ready to take on whatever corporate stooge he had booked for dinner tonight, probably with someone gorgeous on his arm.

"I told you when you took the job, you could stay at my condo. I'll call my assistant there in DC and have him arrange for someone to come and get your belongings today, and have the concierge at the building have the keys ready for you. There. Problem solved."

"Problem solved," I echoed softly, leaning my head back, so it hit a little harder than necessary on the wall. Texting Duncan seemed smart at the time, but sliding into the fallback of relying on him to fix my life left a bitter taste in my mouth. Duncan wanted me to stay with him instead of taking this apartment with Veronica in the first place—hindsight was 20/20, right? Instead, I thought if I wasn't going to be completely comfortable with my job or my city, I at least wanted to have some control over my living arrangements. Not my best decision.

"I gotta go. I'll see you tomorrow morning for the welcome call with the other department heads?"

"See you then, Dunc… and… thanks."

"No problem, little brother. There's a great beer store around the corner from my building, it's on New Jersey Ave. Grab something and put it on my tab before you head up."

The line went dead. I looked around with all my worldly possessions stacked around me, waiting for my phone to ping with details on the movers I knew Duncan's assistant would magically procure out of thin air.

Veronica's Boston psychic had been right. Our relationship wasn't ready for a move like the one we had made, and I could sense some self-destruction and a little moping ahead, but knew it would ultimately be for the best. Navy Yard was more my kind of neighborhood than Georgetown, anyway. I hated needing Duncan's help this way, but suddenly, I couldn't wait to be home.

CHAPTER
Two

CHARLOTTE

Had I walked under a ladder, as a black cat crossed my path, broke thirteen mirrors, and then stepped on every crack on the sidewalk? I don't remember doing any of those things, but I must have pissed off the universe somehow. There was no other way for me to accept just how terrible this day had been.

The balls-hot humidity I encountered every time I stepped outside here in the nation's capital greeted me as I left the offices of the Independent Bookstore Alliance. Leslie Knope was not kidding when she called it a "stupid swamp town."

I fired off an SOS text to my best friend as I moved toward the Metro station and let out a sigh of relief when my phone rang a moment later.

"Blaire, thank God. You will not believe the day I've had," I answered in lieu of any formal greeting. We've been best friends since birth.

"Just pretend we're in our favorite armchairs at Ridge Reads, and tell me all about it."

My reflexive smile at the thought of my family's small bookstore in Holly Ridge faded from my face as I remembered how tense things were between my parents and me, given the fact I was anywhere but home right now.

"You're not actually anywhere near my parents right now, right? They do not need any more ammunition to add to the come-home-and-fulfill-your-family-duty fire right now."

"No, no. I promise. I'm at home waiting for Cole to get back from some meeting or another. No prying ears anywhere around. Hit me with the day." Cole was Blaire's boyfriend of almost two years. They were practically perfect together. It could make one sick, and extremely jealous, if you looked too close for too long.

I let out another rush of air as I wondered where to begin.

"Well, it started off with me being late thanks to a damn Metro delay. I didn't realize I should budget in extra time for trains not to run on schedule. We have one stop light in town!"

"Oh, no. I'm sorry, Char. I know how much you hate being late. But surely they understand you can't control the timing of public transportation?"

"Maybe they could have, but then I followed that performance up with spilling my new boss's coffee all over my good luck silk shirt, and then being ten minutes late to an all-staff meeting because I got the conference room number wrong. Plus, there's a different password for every system I need access to, all with different requirements. I share my cubicle area with someone who enjoys hard-boiled eggs for apparently every meal, and I can't remember the name of anyone I met today."

I felt my eyes prick with tears, the sidewalk and other commuters around me blurring, but I would not be that girl who cried on the Metro her first day in a big city, and I knew if I got started, I wouldn't be able to stop.

"Well, fuck, babe, that is not a good day. There's no way around it, but it is just one day, and tomorrow is a whole new one. If I know you, you're going to be two trains earlier than you need to be, wear something black to hide any potential new food stains, and make up hilarious ways to remember everyone's name tonight so you're set to kill it on day two. You just need a bubble bath and some wine tonight."

Blaire's comforting words didn't help stem the tears that were now falling from my eyes and slowly rolling down my cheeks. We had been apart when Blaire went to college and I stayed home to work at the bookstore, and while she was making a name for herself in the small-town festival circuit. The difference was I had been home and now I was suddenly very much not home.

"Thanks, Blaire. You're right. I printed out the train schedule before I left the office and emailed myself the link to the company directory to start memorizing names and faces. I think I just needed to talk it out. I'll let you get back to heating up your sexy times chocolate fudge."

"We tried that one time!" Blaire said, trying to sound indignant, but failing to succeed as her laughter carried through the connection to my ear.

I felt myself laughing as well, suddenly feeling lighter, but definitely in need of a bath and wine, stat.

"Everything's okay with you all?" I asked.

"Yup, same old here. Spent my day setting up the execution binder for this year's holiday festival, so you know it was a good day. Though Austin is over at our place a lot more now that you're gone. I may need to send him to your place via express mail sometime soon."

I laughed. Austin was Cole's best friend. Our bond had started because our best friends were dating each other, but the resulting friendship was very real.

"I'll keep an eye out for that delivery notification. I'm almost at the Metro now, so I better hang up."

"I'll talk to you soon, Charlotte, okay? Let me know how things go tomorrow. I'll be sending you good vibes. Love you."

"Thanks, Blaire. Love you too."

I slid my phone into my bag, wiping the last of the tears from under my eyes as I descended into the Metro station. Taking a moment to place my earbuds firmly in my ears, I pressed play on today's audiobook. I tapped my SmarTrip card on the reader and found my way to the platform where my train was just arriving. Maybe my luck was turning around.

I found an open seat, even during the evening rush, and sat looking out the window at the darkened tunnel as the train moved toward my condo's stop. I felt a touch dramatic about how upset I had been over my day, but Blaire wasn't wrong when she said I hated to be late. I also hate looking unprepared or feeling like I've failed at something. And while I was feeling dramatic, it truly seemed as if the weight of my world depended on this internship going well. I had given up a lot to be in this city at all right now. That's not saying bridges have already been burned, but one could say the kindling is set at the bottom of the trestles, ready to send them up in flames. Regardless, for once, it was time to bet on myself and I was here to write my own chapter in the book world. I was proud of myself for taking the chance and settled on manifesting a better day for tomorrow.

Exiting the Metro, I realized I'd zoned out through several minutes of the book one of my currently nameless coworkers had recommended at lunch. I would need to rewind, so I didn't get lost. I'd be sure to look up her name first, in case she asked about it tomorrow. Turning the corner, I started the last block toward my borrowed condo in the Navy Yard neighborhood of Southeast DC. Not even my terrible, horrible, no good, very bad day could stop me from appreciating the bustling neighborhood I would spend the next four months in. Gentrification had taken this area over in the last fifteen years and the result was high-rise apartment and condo buildings all around. The neighborhood boasted close access to the city's baseball and soccer stadiums and all the hip—and for my budget, overpriced—bars and restaurants a thirty-something could want.

I waved myself into the lobby, feeling the rush of AC blow as I stepped onto the dark marble floors of the modern-looking space. I waved hello to the concierge. The promise of a cold shower to wash the sweat and the smell of coffee off my body kept me moving.

"Good evening, Ms. Reid. How was your day?" the concierge greeted me, as I made my way past his desk, where he sorted packages from the day's deliveries.

"Hiya, Herold. It definitely could have been better, but I'm glad to be back inside in the AC," I responded.

"It's a hot one today for sure, and only going to be hotter tomorrow. Looks like we'll get a break by the weekend, though."

"Well, thank goodness for that. Have a nice night, sir!" I waved goodbye and walked around the corner to the elevator.

I could never have afforded a closet in this building, or even one in a different neighborhood that came with a concierge on my intern stipend alone, but my mom was talking about my internship one day at the bookstore—complaining about it more likely. Margaret Hayes happened to be there to pick up her newest cozy mystery, and it turned out her oldest stepson, Duncan Brandt, had a condo here in DC. He would be abroad completing business deals across Europe—casual, I know—and folks from Holly Ridge helped their own. I felt guilty taking a connection I knew only came up because mom was info dumping on innocent bystanders about my "abandoning the family business," but also, did I mention I'm a thirty-something living on an intern stipend? Not really a time to be picky.

Entering the elevator, I glimpsed my reflection in the shiny chrome doors. My blond hair, which this morning had been in a sleek, straight, shoulder-length style, was now a stringy, limp mess. I glanced at my button nose, but quickly moved on to notice how red my cheeks were from the oppressive heat. It turns out my mascara had smudged from the sweat, giving me a raccoon likeness, which was just awesome. I slumped against the corner of the elevator, the chrome wall cool on my back, just in time for it to ding as I reached the fifteenth floor. The doors slid open, signaling it was time to get my body moving again. The promise of that cold shower, after which I would promptly shock my system by drinking a glass of red wine in a hot bath, got me out of the elevator. It seemed like I could sleep right there, but hopefully, I'd be asleep by eight and could forget this day ever happened.

I dragged myself down the hall and opened the door to unit 1514. The natural light from the late-summer sun poured into the living room from generous windows, even if they looked out onto one of the highways cutting through the district. As I crossed the common space toward the hallway containing the bedrooms, I dug in my bag to find the case for my wireless earbuds. With the way my day was going, I was sure I would drop them in the bath if I tried to continue listening to my audiobook. I'd change to a physical book and hope one of the few paperbacks that had made the journey from New England didn't end up waterlogged by the conclusion of my soak.

Walking down the hallway, I removed my earbuds and dropped the case in my bag. I was wondering if I should have stopped at the fridge for a glass of wine first when a sudden wall of muscle jerked me back to the present. This same hallway was certainly muscle-wall-free this morning when I left. The muscles in question belonged to a man who just so happened to be shirt-less, his body wrapped in a low-slung towel around his hips. His skin was still damp from his very recent shower, and his body wash contained notes of something woodsy and alluring. Why was I noticing his scent? Surely my mind should be on stranger danger instead of trying to dissect shower products.

Shit! Did I enter the wrong condo? I thought to myself while the stranger in my hallway grabbed me to stop me from bouncing backward onto my ass. No, that doesn't make sense. My key unlocked this one. I wrenched myself out of his strong grip and wielded my bag as a weapon, ready to rain hellfire down on this intruder.

"Who the hell are you?! What are you doing here?!" I yelled at the top of my voice. My eyes traveled up the naked, well-sculpted chest. Were those muscles or bones on his shoulders? My brain ground to a halt as I took in quite possibly the most gorgeous man I had ever seen. A chiseled jaw, symmetrical features, and brilliant green eyes set off chocolate brown hair, curling gently as it started to air dry. I took in the fact that the plump lips above a jaw line plastic surgeons should have in their look-books were moving and the eyebrows of this stranger in my hallway were angry.

"Hello?" the mouth seemed to say. "Who the hell am I? I should ask who the hell you are? Why are you in my brother's place? That doesn't seem like the type of outfit you would wear to clean it. Though the state of the clothes sure matches."

Wow. Someone so pretty could become so ugly just by opening his mouth. At least being Duncan's brother gave him a plausible reason for being in the apartment, so I didn't feel like I was in immediate danger. Still, I wasn't sure why he was in the condo, or even more confusingly, almost naked and wet.

"I'm Charlotte."

"Okay, Charlotte, that's one question answered. How about the other one? Why are you here?"

Wow, doesn't give time to breathe, does this one? I let out a frustrated breath, feeling my relaxing evening getting further and further away.

"I'm Charlotte. I know your brother from—well, I've never actually met Duncan, but his stepmom arranged for me to stay here while I'm interning in the city this fall. We're from the same small town in—"

"Wait, you're from Holly Ridge?"

He stepped back as he processed that I had a plausible reason for being where I was. I realized we remained standing in the hallway, with me still holding my bag raised in the air, poised to pummel if necessary, and he was still in only that towel with his arms crossed. I needed wine.

"I'm going to get something to drink. Can I get you something while you get changed?"

I turned to walk back out to the kitchen, setting my bag on top of one of the bar-height chairs at the breakfast bar in the kitchen. Moving to the fridge to take out the bottle of white I had opened the night before. I hoped to quench my thirst and take the edge off at the same time. Suddenly, a very masculine hand reached past me to grab a can of beer off the middle shelf that hadn't been there when I left this morning. I turned around to find myself between a very shirtless Brandt brother and the fridge. He kept intense eye contact with me as he cracked the tab and swallowed half the can in one go. His drinking seemed to draw my eyes like a magnet to the way his throat looked as he took down the cold liquid.

"So, as we've established, I'm Charlotte. And you are..."

"I'm Hayden. I'm staying here."

CHAPTER
Three

HAYDEN

"Look, Hayden, it has been a day. You can't be staying here. I worked it out with your brother—well, your brother's assistant, really—weeks ago that I would have the place until mid-December when my internship was up. She said nothing about me sharing it with you, and I'm really not comfortable sharing with—"

"What was the assistant's name?"

"I think it was Bethany? She hasn't responded to a few questions I asked over the past few days, but—"

"Yeah, that's the thing. My brother can't keep an assistant to save his life. Bethany is long gone, but it seems like she might have earned her departure if she didn't keep records that showed arrangements had already been made to lend the condo to someone else. Bradley is his assistant now. He's the one who had a messenger bring over the keys for me this afternoon after... after it became clear I was going to need some new accommodations. I'm just about to start as the CIO of the US branch of Duncan's company, so he needs me well-rested. I think that means you'll have to go."

Either the wine, the summer sun, or Charlotte's indignation

had given her cheeks an alluring reddish hue, but when her blue eyes met mine, I felt ice in my veins. Indignation it was, then.

"Well, Mr. CIO, I'm pretty sure it's in the company's best interests, and considering the paycheck they surely pay you, for you to find another place to live. Meanwhile, my intern pay won't cover anything within a forty-minute Metro ride of my office and all intern housing will be full for the semester. Don't make me call Margaret, Hayden."

Hit a man where it hurts, why don't you? My stepmom would deliver a smack upside my head the next time she saw me if I pushed this woman out onto the street when she was obviously trying to make a go of something in her life. She had changed the Brandt family for the better when she met and married my dad thirteen years ago. I'd have to come up with another solution.

"Okay, fine. It's too late today anyway to do something about it. I'll email Duncan and have him call me at the ass-crack of dawn, or whenever, since he's hours ahead of us on European time. But where's all your stuff? I didn't see it in the master bedroom?"

Charlotte picked up the wine bottle and her glass, starting to walk backward toward the hallway, apparently content she had won this round. "I'm a guest in this house. I'm in the guest room, of course. Now, if you'll excuse me, it's been a clusterfuck of a day, and the tub in the guest bath is calling my name."

At this, she swiveled around and stomped off to the guest room, slamming the door shut with what I considered a bit more force than necessary, and locked her door with an audible click. Only at this point did it sink in I just had a stand-off with a complete stranger in my brother's kitchen, in a city I didn't really want to be in, hours after a psychic decided the fate of my relationship, all while wearing a bath towel around my waist.

"It's time to get your shit together, Brandt," I muttered to myself, as I grabbed two more beers from the fridge and made my way back to Duncan's room to put some real clothes on. I may be a

guest too, but he was my brother, and I intended to make myself at home here in his place. Chinese takeout, baseball, and beers on the couch sounded like just what the doctor ordered for tonight. Dealing with the wild cat blond down the hall could wait until tomorrow. I had to admit, though, I didn't quite feel the need to sulk any longer.

Text Interlude

DUNCAN (4:13 AM)

H, I got your email. Fucking Bethany. I can't believe she screwed this one up this badly.

Margaret mentioned someone from Holly Ridge needing a place to stay, so I had her go through Bethany for the details and I never heard another thing about it.

HAYDEN (4:15 AM)

So you were fucking her when she was there?

DUNCAN (4:17 AM)

Real mature, Hayden. You know I don't dip my pen in the company ink… anymore.

HAYDEN (4:18 AM)

Why are you texting and not calling me? I set an alarm for 4 am so I'd be awake.

DUNCAN (4:19 AM)

On my way to a meeting and I'm booked in the quiet car of the train. So, the girl says she has nowhere to go?

HAYDEN (4:21 AM)

The girl is Charlotte. And yeah, she said she's an intern and said something about her stipend and trouble finding anything affordable... I don't know. It was at the end of a very long day.

DUNCAN (4:23 AM)

Got it. I can't believe she threatened to call Margaret. This girl's got some balls.

HAYDEN (4:25 AM)

You're not kidding. I thought she was going to attack me with her handbag when we *literally* ran into each other in the hallway last night. They almost retracted into my body from fear.

DUNCAN (4:27 AM)

So, do you want me to have Bradley find you somewhere else to stay?

HAYDEN (4:28 AM)

No way, I'm not moving AGAIN. I'll just find a way to... convince her to leave.

DUNCAN (4:29 AM)

If I get any sort of text, call, or carrier pigeon from Margaret, that you've pissed this girl off. You're on charity committee duty for 3 months.

HAYDEN (4:31 AM)

Charity duty? That's for interns!

DUNCAN (4:33 AM)

Well, you're living with one, so you'll be ready to get on their level. Be nice, Hayden.

HAYDEN (4:34 AM)

zipped lip emoji

CHARLOTTE (6:53 AM)

I need your help to get rid of a toweled intruder in my otherwise peaceful condo.

AUSTIN (6:54 AM)

Uh, shouldn't you call the cops for that?

CHARLOTTE (6:59 AM)

Okay, intruder isn't quite the right word. It's Hayden Brandt, Duncan's brother. Apparently, there was a mix-up, and he thinks he's staying here too. He needs to go.

AUSTIN (7:01 AM)

What are you thinking?

CHARLOTTE (7:05 AM)

I need to dig into your prankster past.

AUSTIN (7:07 AM)

Pranks and gossip. My specialty. FaceTime tonight?

CHARLOTTE (7:09 AM)

You're the best BFF-boyfriend's-BFF I could have ever asked for. Talk to you at 7?

AUSTIN (7:10 AM)

Dancing Girls Emoji *Dancing Boys Emoji*

CHAPTER
Four

CHARLOTTE

I cracked open my bedroom door and peeked into the hall-way. I listened hard for a moment, but didn't hear signs of anyone moving around in the kitchen or living room. It seemed either Hayden was a late riser, or he had already left for the day. Opening the door the rest of the way, I carefully made my way to the front door, walking lightly so my shoes didn't make any sound on the hardwood floor. Thankfully, the office had a coffee machine in the kitchen. I wasn't ready to risk another encounter with my *roomie* before I had caffeine.

After the doors closed on the elevator, taking me toward day two of my internship, I breathed a sigh of relief and placed my earbuds in my ears. I was, in fact, about thirty minutes earlier than I needed to be, but I planned to use the time on the train to recenter and prepare to make today a million times better than yesterday. I wore my lucky jade wrap dress, one that managed to hug my curves, yet stay professional. The dress choice was entirely due to wanting some extra luck for a better second day, not at all in case I ran into any unexpected condo-sharers, shirtless or not, between my room and the building's exit.

As I opened the front door to the building, I looked at my phone to confirm the train schedule and stopped just short of running into a muscled wall again. This time, the muscles were covered with a grey shirt and gym shorts, the shirt soaked through and darkened with sweat. I could tell from the woodsy scent it was Hayden before I lifted my head to make eye contact.

When had I scent-marked him? Not good, Charlotte.

"Charlotte," he said, nodding his head in greeting as he grabbed the door from me and held it open so I could pass.

"Hayden," I responded, forcing myself to keep my eyes on his face and not follow the trail a bead of sweat created down his cheek and to the collar of his shirt. This backfired on me when I realized I had been staring *and* blocking the doorway for longer than was socially polite. I jerked into motion, brushing past him and schooling myself to not look back as I walked toward the Metro station.

Okay, my apartment interloper was criminally hot, and apparently worked to keep himself that way. That was an objective fact, like the sky was blue and water was wet. Austin and I would find a way to get under his skin, all the same. And if he happened to notice how good my ass looked in this dress, well, that was a bonus.

For now, it was time to forget about Mr. Brandt and focus on... focusing.

As my train arrived at the stop closest to the Independent Bookseller Alliance, known colloquially as the IBA, I felt much calmer and more prepared than I had yesterday. In part, it was because I realized that today couldn't go much worse than yesterday had. By odds alone, it had to be better.

After a quick walk from the station to Gallery Place, the building that housed the offices of the IBA, I put my stuff down at my desk and noticed I had some time to kill before my first meeting of the day. Time to get the caffeine I skipped while trying to avoid Hayden this morning.

I was making my latte in the kitchen when Marta—thank goodness for that company directory—entered.

"Hi, Charlotte. Happy second day!"

"Thanks, Marta! I started listening to that thriller you recommended yesterday. It's really creepy! Makes me glad I'm not at home in my small town right now. I think I slept better knowing I'm in the big, scary city."

Marta smiled at me.

"Well, let me know when you're done with that one. I've got a ton more to recommend."

"I definitely will. I prefer romance novels over anything else, but really want to give more genres a try while I'm working here, see if I can become a more well-rounded reader."

"I'll definitely take any romance recommendation you have. I could use a break from the murder books once in a while. So, what brings you to the big, scary city and the IBA?"

I thought for a second about how honest and transparent to be with this virtual stranger, even one I could see becoming a friend. I had laid it all out on my application. Part of the reason I got the internship, I think. Why not see if it resonated more widely as well?

"I'm from a small town in New England where my parents run an independent bookstore. I didn't go to college right after high school, so I could stay home and help them run it. I love them, and I love Ridge Reads, don't get me wrong, but I have this feeling like I could be doing *more*, ya know? I love the idea of working with books forever, but don't necessarily love the idea of never leaving the town and life I was born into. So, when I saw the chance open up to work with the IBA's Bookstore Future Fund, I jumped at it. My background is in PR and marketing, so the fundraising is going to be new, but I'm excited about it."

Marta nodded along the whole time I talked, and when I

finished to take a breath and sip the coffee that was cooling in my hands, she broke into a large grin.

"I could sense a real 'books' person in you. It's no surprise at all that Paula gave you the job. You'll learn a ton working for her, even if the work is hard."

I felt myself smiling back at my new work friend.

"That's what I'm hoping. Speaking of Paula, I better get back to my cube to be sure I'm prepped for our one-on-one this morning. Maybe we can get lunch sometime this week?"

"That sounds like a plan. I'll message you. Have a great morning, Charlotte."

I exited the kitchen, walking back toward my desk, taking in my coworkers as they started to arrive for the day. The walls of the hallways and conference rooms were lined with photos of different independent bookstores across the country that belonged to the IBA.

I wonder if Ridge Reads is pictured here anywhere. I'll have to keep an eye out.

I reviewed the onboarding documentation I had been set up with yesterday until the meeting reminder went off for my check in with Paula Lapman, the Vice President for New Initiatives at the IBA and the head of the Bookstore's Future Fund. Paula's tenure with the IBA spanned over thirty years and she was a bit of a legend in the indie bookstore community. I was excited to work with her.

I nodded to her assistant, Raúl, and knocked on her door at 9:00 a.m. sharp.

"Come in," I heard from within the office.

Pushing the door gently, I took in the corner office on the third floor. The windows looked out on the bustling streets below, showing four exercise studios, three coffee shops, and two bakeries, just in the immediate frame of view. Paula's office looked how I imagined an editor's office would appear, with bookshelves artistically lined with books, photos of Paula and major players in the literary industry, and a comfy couch and chairs combo in the corner. Paula stood up from her desk as I crossed the threshold and indicated toward that space. I sat down in one of the blue suede chairs, while she moved toward the opposite one.

"Good morning, Charlotte. Glad to see you back on day two. How was your first day?"

Filtering had never been a strong suit of mine, and before I could stop myself, I was laughing a bit maniacally and covering my face with my hands.

"Well, honestly, Ms. Lapman, it was a bit of a disaster."

Paula nodded gently, settling back into her chair as she appraised me from six feet away.

"I sensed a bit of a defeated air from you when I walked past your cubical toward the end of the day yesterday. Plus, I couldn't help but notice the brown stain on your shirt didn't seem to be an intentional fashion choice. Tell me, Charlotte, have you heard tales of my first day at the IBA yet?"

"I can't say I have, Ms. Lapman," I said, somewhat warily. *Where was she going with this?*

"Please, call me Paula."

I nodded, eager for her to continue.

"It was the early 1990s, and I was coming to the IBA from a bookseller background, like many of our employees do. I hadn't hidden in my interview that I would be moving here with my partner, now wife, and our young child. This ruffled some feathers, so I was already highly anxious. This was my dream job, but I wasn't about to hide who I was to have it. To make a long story short, I ended up calling my boss by the wrong name all day, and no one bothered to correct me. I considered not coming back the next day, but knew I had something to contribute and, even more so, something to prove to the doubters and to myself. Sound like anyone you know?"

I nodded again, dumbstruck that this powerful woman was sharing something so personal with me.

"Thank you, Ms... Paula. Just... thank you."

Paula smiled gently, before morphing her face into an expression that showed personal bonding time was over, and she was ready to be all business once more.

"All right, then. So, shake yesterday off, and let's get down to work. Let's start by discussing the Storybook Ball Gala that will be happening near the end of October."

CHAPTER
Five

HAYDEN

The car service Duncan added me to pulled up in front of 525 Massachusetts Avenue to deliver me to my first day of work at Brandt Investing International headquarters. The evening of baseball and beers wasn't quite enough to erase the rest of yesterday's altercations, which, combined with the apprehension of this first day, made for a hell of a case of insomnia. I hadn't even needed the alarm I set for four, so I could talk to Duncan as he started his day. After the disappointing text exchange, I lay there staring at the ceiling fan above the king bed before dragging myself out at six to go for a run. It was at the end of that run I found myself greeted by Charlotte exiting our building much earlier than I expected her to leave.

I barely took in the granite tile floors and sterile white walls brightened with run-of-the-mill wall sconces, as I flashed my badge to the security guard waiting inside the building's front doors and crossed to the bank of elevators. I thought instead of my brief run-in with my *temporary* roommate. She seemed to have shaken off her bad day better than I had, looking like she was ready to eat a man for breakfast as she power-walked through the lobby to the front door. I'm not sure what compelled me to wait for her to exit, but when she looked up at me, inches away from her face meeting my chest *again*, her eyes had taken on a green tint from her dress.

The sound of the elevator doors opening on the fourth floor brought me back to the present. Waiting for me at the end of the elevator's hallway was Leslie, the administrative assistant Duncan had assigned to get me up to speed on operations around the office. We had met briefly via video call last week, but it surprised me to find her greeting me straight off the elevator.

"Good morning, Mr. Brandt," she said, handing me the waiting cup of coffee in her right hand.

"Good morning, Leslie. Hayden is fine. I wouldn't want to scare anyone by thinking Duncan has returned from across the pond earlier than planned."

Leslie chuckled politely. She gestured to the right, indicating the direction we should move and fell in step next to me.

"I hope you weren't waiting there for me long, Leslie. I can only assume you have better things to do with your time. Thanks for the coffee, by the way. Not to be *that boss*, but can you tell me what's in it?"

"Your driver gave me a ring after you got out of the car, and it's an Americano with a splash of oat milk. I tracked down your old assistant in Boston with Mr. Brandt's help and got her to give me a list of some of your favorites. Not a dairy allergy, but a preference when it comes to coffee. It's all locked up here." Leslie tapped her temple and pointed at the office right in front of us.

What I assumed was her desk sat in a vestibule, with an open door directly behind it, setting her up as a gatekeeper of sorts. I could tell she would be an efficient one, already laughing at my bad jokes and sourcing out my coffee preferences all on her own. My old assistant, Danielle, was good, but nothing like this.

I found myself comparing Leslie's dark ringlet curls to blond hair that fell to one's shoulder in waves. *Snap out of it, Brandt. Charlotte will be gone before you know it, and you need to stop further connecting yourself to anything and everything Duncan throws in your lap, accidentally or intentionally.*

I looked up to see Leslie looking at me curiously and realized I had stopped even with her desk, about eight feet away from the office door I should have continued to. I smiled the disarming Brandt smile at her as I continued into the office, noting the nameplate that read "Hayden Brandt, Chief Information Officer" as I entered.

"There's an ample budget to order any additional furniture or supplies you may need to make this office your own, Hayden. I have some catalogs out here if you need them, or I can make some suggestions if you describe what you might need and your preferred style. We'll make you feel at home here before you know it."

As I gazed out the window at the grid of streets and buildings below us, I thought how unlikely I was to feel settled in a place so urban and impersonal. But I was here. I made a commitment, and one thing Duncan had taught me was that we kept our word to each other.

"Thanks, Leslie. I'll probably see how things flow over the next few weeks before committing to anything major, to make sure I'm not purchasing anything too rashly. I'm guessing when I open my desk drawer, I'm going to find my favorite pens, notebooks, and sticky notes, so I'll be good to get started for the day."

Leslie looked pleased with my observation of her attention to detail.

"Prudent, just like Mr. Brandt. I look forward to our work together, Hayden. All your access information is on your desk there. Shall I let you get settled, and then we can review your schedule in about thirty minutes?"

"That sounds great, Leslie. Thank you."

She nodded and turned around, walking back to her desk. I couldn't see her from this angle, but I could hear the gentle clack of her keyboard and the quiet ring of her phone as she greeted the caller on the other end.

I walked behind the desk set in the far corner of the room, putting the cityscape to my back as I sat in the chair and slid into the long wooden side. Picking up the well-organized access document, I logged into my new computer, immediately changing the password—old habits die hard—and set to work. Information systems comforted me, and throwing myself into managing a new one would help me feel comfortable, even as I longed for open space instead of a concrete jungle around me. Duncan had expectations for me, and even after all these years, few things motivated me more.

K*nock, knock*
I looked up from the report I had been reviewing on system security Duncan had ordered after the last CIO's departure, expecting Leslie, but instead found my older brother, Preston.

"Still good for lunch today, Hay?"

"Shit! Is it lunchtime already?"

Preston smiled at me knowingly. "I'd be offended if I didn't also regularly work through lunch. Come on. Let me take you somewhere in the neighborhood that you'll ask Leslie to order from regularly."

I got up and greeted Preston with a hug. While I wasn't necessarily thrilled with relocating to another big city, being in the same city with more of my brothers was a definite bonus.

"Are you taking him to Founding Farmers?" Leslie asked as we pulled even with her desk, heading toward lunch.

"Yup, for the dumplings," Preston replied.

"That was my guess! Danielle said they were his favorite working late treat." Leslie looked back and forth between us.

"You're not Hayden's twin, though, right? I didn't think he lived in the city, but now seeing you together..."

"You're admitting you don't know something, Leslie. I'm shocked," I responded, smiling to let her know I was joking. "Preston is between Hunter, my twin, and I and Duncan in birth order. Preston often got confused for our triplet growing up. Our youngest brother, Spencer, looks like a scrawnier Duncan."

"That was my mistake for the day, Hayden. I promise. Now, go on and enjoy your lunch. That way I can get to mine," Leslie responded.

Yup, only four hours into our day, and I had to admit Duncan was right. She would be a perfect assistant for me.

Preston and I made our way to the elevators.

"So, you said you had a story to tell me today?" Preston asked as he hit the down button to call the car.

"Nope, definitely not telling that story in my brand-new place of work. How's the Senate?"

As we rode down to the first floor and walked the few blocks to the restaurant, Preston caught me up on his job as the Chief of Staff for one of the senators from Rhode Island.

"We're, of course, already looking ahead to reelection next year. It shouldn't be too big of a fight, but the party has lost a few seats in the state house and senate over the past few years, so we don't want to get too complacent."

"I don't think anyone could ever accuse you of complacency, Prez," I teased, using the nickname we gave Preston after the first time he stayed up on election night until way past his bedtime coloring in a copy of the map as the Electoral College results were called. No one who knew Preston growing up would have doubted he'd end up exactly where he was. The real question was when he would run for office himself.

Preston smiled in good humor as he grabbed the door to the restaurant, ushering me in ahead of him. The smell of freshly prepared food hit my nose, and suddenly, my stomach growled.

The Americano of this morning no longer served as a sufficient breakfast.

"Welcome! Lunch for two?" the hostess greeted us as we approached her stand.

"Yes, please. We should have a reservation under Brandt," Preston replied.

"Ah, yes. Welcome, Mr. Brandt. Follow me right this way."

We followed the redhead to a two-top table in the back of the restaurant against a wall decorated with dark-stained wood and away from the main traffic flow. The perfect place to regale Preston with the events of my life over the past twenty-four hours.

Preston was still laughing as the waiter brought back our waters, struggling to get ahold of himself.

"We're going to need a minute," I said to the poor guy, who looked bewildered as tears streamed down Preston's face.

"All right, all right, I don't know that it's *that* funny."

"Oh, but it is, Hay. She lawyered your ass at the same time she kicked said ass to the curb based on the advice of her psychic. I know I was busy with the midterms and all, but I wondered why I never met her over the past year. I guess that explains it."

I sat with that for a moment. Veronica and I hadn't lived all that far away from everyone in Boston, but he was right. She had somehow never met any of my brothers, let alone Dad and Margaret.

"I guess I owe Madam London something, after all. I hate having to crash in Duncan's place though, especially because it came partially occupied."

I paused here in my story, placing our order for dumplings and drunken noodles and digging into the bread basket the waiter supplied on his return trip.

"Wait. What do you mean the apartment is occupied?" Preston continued as the waiter walked away to place our orders with the kitchen.

"Duncan's previous assistant fucked up and offered the place to someone from Holly Ridge needing a place while she completes her internship. Margaret made the connection."

"Oh, Duncan and his assistants. And if Margaret is involved, you—"

"Can't just kick the girl out," I finished the sentence.

"So, what are you going to do?"

"Well, I didn't exactly make the best first impression. I may have baited her and then chugged a beer wearing only my towel."

Preston choked on his water.

"That's definitely... an image."

"I had just been kicked out of my home and then found a stranger claiming *she* was living in the condo I expected to be living in alone. It wasn't my finest moment."

"So, again, I ask, what are you going to do?" Preston said as our food arrived.

"I'm not really sure. I mean, I'd rather not have a roommate, but she seems harmless enough. She seemed to have picked herself up after having a bad day yesterday. If we're both busy with work, what does it matter if we're sleeping in separate rooms?"

"So, it's a she, huh? A pretty she?" Preston asked slyly, cutting into his noodles.

"She's a she. Just a body. In the condo I'm living in *for now*. I'll need to find another place when Duncan gets back from Europe anyway, so what could a few months hurt?"

Preston looked at me in that smug way only older brothers have.

"Oh, I think it could hurt a lot."

I rolled my eyes at him as I picked up my silverware and dug into my own lunch.

"Eat your noodles, Prez."

He laughed through a mouthful of dumplings, looking entirely too pleased in my misery.

CHAPTER
Six

CHARLOTTE

Arriving back at the condo after a successful second day, I was pleased things seemed back on track. Paula caught me up on the progress for the Storybook Ball Gala and handed a lot of the remaining planning off to me. It would be a busy time finishing everything off, but I was excited about the prospect of the money we raise and what it could do for the future of independent bookstores.

Walking into the kitchen, I jumped at the movement I caught out of the corner of my eye.

"Evening, Charlotte," Hayden greeted me, his voice deep and silky. He twisted the cap off a bottle of beer, still wearing his jacket, shirt, and tie from the office this morning.

Right. My *roommate*. How could I have forgotten?

"Hey, Hayden," I responded, as my eyes took in the way his jacket fit those broad shoulders. So far, I had known Hayden for twenty-four hours, and already I knew he looked fantastic in a towel, delicious in a sweaty grey T-shirt, and downright sinful in a suit. Plus, if I thought him swallowing down beer from a can was alluring, those lips wrapped around a bottle of beer was off the charts. I needed to find a flaw in this man, and quickly.

"See you managed to keep your outfit coffee-free today. Great job," Hayden smirked as he lifted the bottle to his lips.

Ricgggght. He's a cocky stepson of a lovely woman doing me a favor. That'll do.

"My day was great, thanks. How was yours?" I responded as I crossed to the fridge to pull out my wine. Apparently, it was happy hour in our humble little abode.

"It wasn't half bad. My brother assigned a great assistant to work with me to help me get settled. I had lunch with another one of my brothers. He took me to Founding Farmers, which had some amazing dumplings. They're my favorite."

I blinked at him, pausing mid-pour. I hadn't expected a real answer, let alone for Hayden to share something so detailed about himself. Was this a trick?

Recovering, I responded, "Founding Farmers? I've heard of them. I think there's one not too far from my office in Gallery Place. Though I've heard great things about their mac and cheese, which is definitely my comfort food."

"Gallery Place, huh? I don't think that's too far from Duncan's offices either."

We both sipped our drinks in silence for a moment before Hayden broke it again.

"I realized I never asked last night, what internship are you here for?"

I took another sip. This personality switch was a bit unnerving. I thought I had him pegged as a cocky asswipe and now he's showing interest in me?

"I'm working for the Independent Bookstore Alliance on their Independent Bookstore Future Fund. It raises money that indie bookstores can apply for in grants when they hit on hard times; the owner gets sick or something happens to the bookstore space or the inventory itself. Amazon is expected to control eighty percent of the book market in just a few years, and bookstores like these are so important for the community.

It's important they have resources to fall back on to get them back on their feet."

Hayden nodded, his eyes intent on my face, taking in the words I'm saying. Intense listener, this one.

"That does sound really important. There's this great bookstore in Holly Ridge... well, I'm sure you know it. You grew up there. Margaret just loves it."

I felt myself turn slightly red at the mention of Ridge Reads.

"That's actually my family's store. I've been working there since I could reach the register. You're right, it's great. But I dunno, I wanted to do something more..."

Hayden looked at me with a million more questions in his eyes, and I found myself unable to look away. I didn't necessarily want to live with someone who made me feel such a mix of emotions—hate, lust, annoyance—for several months, but I definitely wasn't comfortable with the pull I was feeling to this friendlier, more open version of Hayden. A noise broke into my consciousness, and after a few seconds, I realized my phone was buzzing from where it sat on the kitchen island between us. We both looked down, and I saw Austin's name, with a picture of him carrying me on his back displayed, as he called me for our scheduled FaceTime date.

I looked back up at Hayden's face and saw the interest fade that was in his eyes a moment ago. It didn't take a genius to recognize he was assuming Austin was someone significant to me, and for some reason, I didn't bother to correct him.

"I should get this," I said, as I reached for the phone and picked up my glass of wine.

Hayden nodded, taking a deep pull from his beer bottle, but saying nothing more.

"Hey, Austin," I greeted, as I retreated toward my bedroom, smiling as his handsome face appeared on the screen.

"Hey, Charlie-cakes, how goes it?"

I shut the door to my bedroom behind me.

"Oh, it goes. Much better day today than yesterday. How are you? Tell me a good story while I get changed?"

I sat the phone down on top of my dresser, so Austin was looking at the ceiling, while I pulled sweats and a loose crop-top T-shirt out of it to change into.

"I have a third date with Mitch tonight, so it's time to decide whether I'm really into him or just a little bored."

"What's wrong with this one?" I asked as I pulled the tie on my dress.

"Well, he has big ears for one thing."

A laugh rocketed out of me.

"Big ears? Really, Austin?"

"What? His hair is too short, so they really stick out from his head! You forget about Madeline from last month, with her big eyes. Apparently, I'm just working my way through too large facial features. He is a nice guy, though. Maybe the ears won't look so big tonight."

I picked the phone back up so I could see Austin's face, noting his eyes are a little sad while his tone is light.

"Or maybe you're just looking for excuses to end things before someone gets too close?" I offered, my tone warm, yet serious.

I caught a glimpse of pain roll over his features before he visibly shrugged it off and deflected.

"Enough psychoanalysis, book girl. Let's get down to you and your issues. How's the roomie today?"

I glanced toward the door, wondering if Hayden was still in the kitchen and just how far Austin's loud voice might carry.

"He's... interesting. He was a complete prick last night, which is why I texted you, but today, he was actually interested in my internship and the work I'm passionate about? I dunno. Maybe he just needed the endorphins from his run this morning—"

"Oh, Mr. Roomie is a runner? Does he only focus on leg day, or does he remember arm day too?"

I rolled my eyes widely, making sure Austin picked up on the gesture.

"So *not* the point, friend. In any case, I don't know, this evening seemed different. Maybe it wouldn't be so bad sharing the space? It's only until December anyway and it seems like his job is pretty high-level and will keep him plenty occupied."

"Wait, what is this? You're giving into sharing the space with him? This look of acquiescence is new on you... Do you *like* him? That's new on you too. You know, in the almost two years of our friendship, I have really held up my end of the dating stories while you have lived like a nun..."

I held up a hand, trying to stop this A-train before it ran off the rails.

"Stop, stop. It's nothing like that. It's his brother's place. He has a claim to it too, and his brother only said I could stay here because Margaret intervened. It's just not my place to rock the boat. And it might be kinda nice to know someone in the city. Have someone who knows when I get home and knows where I come from and all that."

"It might also be *nice* to have someone lick out the cobwebs from your ..."

"Oh, look at that, Mom's calling. Gotta go!" I interjected as my phone buzzed, the call waiting notification appearing at the top of the screen, stopping Austin from saying the rest of that sentence. Unfortunately, there was no stopping the image from popping into my mind.

"Convenient timing, Mrs. Reid," Austin said, a devilish look on his face. "Tell her I said hi, and let me know if you need this prank document. I spent a good hour compiling it during my shift this afternoon."

"Will do. Love you, A."

"Love you right back, Charlie Brown."

The smile from another one of Austin's ridiculous nicknames faded as I clicked on the answer button for my mom's phone call.

"Hi, Mom,"

"Charlotte, hello. I assume you got settled all right?"

I guess I had "forgotten" to call after I got all my stuff settled a few days ago.

"Yeah, Mom. I did. Sorry I didn't call. It's just been a busy few days figuring out my route to work, buying a Metro card, finding the store, and all that. You know how it goes."

"A perk of never moving out of the town you were born in is you never have to worry about any of that."

I winced. I set her up for that one.

"How's the store?" I asked, knowing it was a double-edged sword. I wasn't sure I really wanted to know, but I also knew it would hurt her deeply if I didn't ask.

"Things are fine. We hired another girl to take over your shifts. The first one you trained quit. Something about the Point-of-Sale system being too hard to manage. Hopefully this new one will stick."

"You know, if you considered one of the new POS systems I got the demos for, it might be a little more user-friendly and would allow us to take online orders and—"

"It's all right. It's just for four months and then you'll be back in time for the last few weeks of the holiday rush. We'll stumble through until then."

I tried to hold in a sigh as we rehashed the same conversation for the fiftieth time since I told her about the internship.

"Well, that could be true, Mom, but remember, I'm really hoping the internship will turn into a job offer, which would mean—"

"All right, well, I've got to go. Mrs. Morris just walked in and needs her new Harlequin serial for the week. Talk to you soon. Stay safe."

"Bye, Mom," I finished weakly, the silence coming from the other end of the line louder than any of the words she said to me. I flopped back against my pillows, huffing out a breath. She didn't understand why this was important to me, and it seemed like she wasn't willing to. Ridge Reads had greatly benefited from the same program I was working for, helping to fill in funding gaps during the pandemic. I represented the third generation of Ridge Reads and I loved the store, but my parents' unwillingness to grow and change with the times had stifled my ability to see myself there long term. If they didn't act fast, there wouldn't be a Ridge Reads for me to take over when they retired, and I knew there were plenty of other stores across the country like it.

Suddenly, I heard the shower in the master across the hall start up. *How many showers does this guy take in twenty-four hours?* The image of Hayden in a towel, then dropping the towel, then stepping into the shower, jumped into my mind.

I sat up in my bed suddenly. No, absolutely not. Austin was right. I had lived somewhat like a nun ever since he'd known me, and even before, but there was a reason, and I was so close to getting it. I had gotten my degree while working full time at the store. I had upset my parents and put the store even more at risk by leaving, even if it was just for a few months. I couldn't let anything distract me from my goals.

I picked up my phone and opened to my text thread with Austin.

CHARLOTTE (8:25 PM)

I need that prank document, please and thank you. He's gotta go.

AUSTIN (8:26 PM)

Already in your email. Chat with Mom not go well?

CHARLOTTE (8:29 PM)

It was... more of the same. But, thanks for sending it. You get me.

AUSTIN (8:01 PM)

Anytime. Let me know how some of these go over, and you know, feel free to send pics, so I can see what we're working with *winking emoji* *eggplant emoji*

I navigated over to my email app and pulled up the list Austin sent. It looked like he had emailed it as soon as we hung up, correctly predicting what talking to my mom would do to my mood. He really was a great friend. I started scheming, seeing if there was anything on the list I could implement immediately and began an Amazon cart for the supplies I didn't have. Time for you and your freakishly defined shoulders to find somewhere else to shower, Hayden Brandt.

CHAPTER
Seven

HAYDEN

I returned to the apartment after another run along the river. I hadn't seen Charlotte since our conversation in the kitchen last night. I'm sure she had to have eaten dinner at some point, but she was quiet as a mouse about it.

Who was that Austin guy, anyway?

Not that it mattered. We were just temporarily thrown together here, so no use getting attached.

Sure, say it one more time, then it'll really stick.

As I got into the shower and washed off the sweat from the early morning DC humidity, I thought about the way Charlotte's eyes lit up when she was talking about wanting to help other independent bookstores survive and thrive. I could admit that Charlotte was gorgeous, her curves, hair, and blue eyes sparkling, but when those same eyes were lit from inside with her enthusiasm and passion? That was my catnip.

You've had one real conversation with the girl. She's pretty and she's passionate, but what you don't know could be a whole can of worms you don't want to open. Let it go, Brandt.

As I finished washing the shampoo out of my hair, enjoying the excellent water pressure in Duncan's shower that was large enough for six men my size, I tried to do just that. I thought ahead to the day in front of me—more get-to-know-you meetings and reviewing reports. I hated this part of starting a new job. I just wanted to dig into things and get to work. Though, my days of digging through code and systems were likely limited, given the Chief at the front of my new title.

I pulled on another suit, navy blue this time, and added the tie the tailor had suggested I wear with it. I looked at the clock on the bedside table and swore, hating that I was running behind. I'd still arrive at the office before most other people, but doubted I'd beat Leslie.

I walked into the kitchen and grabbed my reusable coffee mug, heading to the machine to brew a quick cup of coffee for the road. My hand immediately detected something sticky along the bottom of the cup.

"What the..." I said as I put the cup back on the counter and examined my hand. "Is that soap?"

I guess the cup had been sitting in some leftover dish soap from when Charlotte had done her dishes last night. I turned on the faucet to rinse off the cup and my hand. All of a sudden, I was doused with a torrent of water as the sprayer came to life, maneuvering out of its perch to cover me from crotch to shoulder and then carried on with soaking the kitchen counter and the floors.

"Fuck!" I yelled, overcoming the initial shock of receiving an extra shower after my clothes were already on. I examined the sprayer head to see how this could happen and noticed the handle was depressed with an elastic blue hair tie. This meant as soon as the sink was turned on, it would spray the unwitting fool standing there. I racked my brain, trying to figure out if there was a way a band could have accidentally made its way there, but no, that was definitely intentional placement.

What the actual fuck? Are we twelve? I thought, as I headed back to my room to change. I guess the navy suit would have to wait for another day. I pulled on khaki pants and the charcoal jacket from yesterday. Probably a little more casual than I would have liked for day number two, but I wasn't risking another suit.

And now I'm really late and still don't have my coffee. I returned to the kitchen sink and removed the hair tie, completing the washing of my cup that I was now convinced had been soaped up on purpose to ensure I used the sink this morning. I set the coffeemaker to brew and grabbed my shoes from the front door, sitting on the couch to tie them while I listened to the hot liquid pour into my metal mug.

My toes met resistance partway into my brown dress shoes. "Come the fuck on," I muttered after another shove of my foot didn't yield different results. Pulling the shoe off and into my lap, I reached into the opening and pulled out crumpled paper towels stuffed into the toes of the shoe. "Not very environmentally friendly of you, Ms. Reid," I muttered, repeating the action on the other shoe and coming away with another piece of paper towel.

With my shoes finally on both feet, I grabbed my cup from the coffeemaker, pouring a splash of oat milk from the fridge and a heavy dash of sugar from the sugar bowl. One unfortunate incident was funny, but two pranks before 8:00 a.m. meant war. One upside to city living was the ability to have supplies delivered to your front door in mere hours. I had grown up with four brothers. Charlotte will never know what hit her.

As I walked to the elevator, I took a sip out of my coffee cup and immediately spit it back out, my hand rushing to my chin to avoid needing a third shirt for the morning due to dribbled coffee. *Salt in the sugar bowl? Make that three pranks.* Oh, it was so on.

I was on edge all morning, waiting to see if she had switched out my oat milk for something dairy-based. It was risky to go back for another cup, sugarless this time, but it was the principle of the thing. I wanted my coffee, from my house, in my mug. The possibility she had switched my creamer hit me later. It turns out Charlotte drew a line in the sand on actually killing me, and since she didn't know if I was allergic or just intolerant, she had left my dairy substitute alone.

Leslie had a sandwich from the deli down the street brought in for lunch, since I was on a conference call with people on three different continents. I had to admit, two days in and DC had the edge on lunch options over Boston. My afternoon flew by in a blur of more reports and tracking the progress of the supplies necessary to start operation payback I had ordered to be delivered to the condo. I imagined the shopper picking up confetti, soy sauce, olive oil, and Sprite, wondering if they were shopping for some weird sex thing. Nope, just a thirty-one-year-old man planning pranks. Rushing out of the office as soon as the clock hit five, I hoped I would beat Charlotte home in time to enact some revenge.

I opened the door to our unit, calling out, "Hello?" and was greeted with silence. Bringing in the bags that had been waiting at the concierge desk, I hurried to my room to hide the supplies and change out of my work clothes. Joggers and a T-shirt were definitely better pranking attire.

I paused outside the door to Charlotte's room and took stock of where life found me: holding a bag of confetti, about to enter the room of a person who was essentially a stranger. How did I get here?

She started it. You had to ride in the elevator to your office with twelve other people because you arrived after 8:30 a.m. She's earned this. Besides, it's harmless.

With that, I pushed open the door to the guest room and yelled her name one more time for good measure, and then I got to work.

CHAPTER
Eight

CHARLOTTE

I got back to the condo a little after six and all I could think about was what I could eat to tide me over until I could get to the store to grab some groceries for dinner. I allowed myself a few days of take-out while I got settled into a new routine, but a quick peak at my bank account today on the Metro reminded me I wouldn't be able to live that lifestyle forever.

I was opening the door to my room, intent on changing out of today's pantsuit, when for the third time this week, I was met with a male chest in my face. Covered in a non-sweaty shirt this time, at least.

"Hayden?" I asked, wondering why he was possibly in my room, with the door closed.

"Oh, hey, Charlotte. Bet you're wondering why I am in your room, huh?"

"You basically read my mind."

"Well, I got home just a little while ago and noticed a squeaking coming from your room. I recognized it as a squeaky ceiling fan, having just tightened the one in my room last night, so I thought I'd fix yours too."

"Squeaky ceiling fan, huh?" I stepped around him and took

stock of my room. Nothing seemed obviously out of place. My bed was still unmade, so he couldn't have put rubber snakes in it. I wasn't sure how Hayden would respond to my morning pranks, but finding him in here made me think it wasn't going to be lying down.

"If that's the case, then where's the screwdriver?" I nodded at his empty hands, dangling at his sides.

"Oh, uhh…"

As Hayden fumbled to come up with a plausible reason why he didn't have a screwdriver in hand, I walked toward the bed and pulled the chain to restart the fan blades. I hadn't noticed a squeak when I left this morning.

The blades of the fan started to turn and rainbow paper confetti fluttered from the ceiling, landing in all corners of my room, with a concentration on my—as previously mentioned—unmade bed. I looked up at the fan in shock and then over at the giant man-child standing in the doorway, doubled over with laughter.

"So, that's how it's going to be, huh, Brandt? Just remember… you went into my room first."

At that, I shouldered past him into the hallway, grabbing my clutch out of my work bag, and stormed out the door. Changing could wait until *after* I grabbed something to eat. Groceries would have to wait, too. Though, I definitely still needed to stop at the store. Suddenly, two-day shipping didn't seem at all fast enough.

The next morning, I was walking to my bathroom in my robe when I heard an aggravated yell from inside Hayden's room. Smiling to myself, I stopped my progress to wait and see if he would come out and yell at me in person or suffer in silence.

The door to his room was wrenched open, and I was blessed by Hayden Brandt in a towel yet again, though the hairless stripe on his otherwise hairy left leg did take away from the larger, sexy package a bit.

I drew my hand up to my mouth to contain my giggles, but when my eyes met his, I could tell he could hear them.

"It's bad enough I pissed all over my feet this morning when I got up, meaning I had to shower right away and skip my run, but *why* is my hair *falling off* my *leg*?"

"You've never heard of the old replace-the-body-wash-with-Nair prank? It's a classic. By the way... you snore."

"I do not!" Hayden spluttered. "I can't believe you came into my room while I was sleeping to shrink-wrap my toilet and mess with my body wash."

"Like I said, Hayden... you came into my room first. And I have to say, you wear the hell out of that towel, but you'd also make Mr. Calvin Klein very proud with that ass in your boxer briefs."

I left him spluttering behind me as I finished my trip to the bathroom and shut the door. I made a mental note to take my shower products to my room every day, and start using that key I found in the doorknob of the spare room when I arrived.

While our pranks were escalating, they remained mostly harmless. He did clean up the stain the soy sauce and Sprite mixture left on the rug under the couch after I did a hell of a spit take when he swapped it out for my Diet Coke. We quickly learned that when we were both home, it seemed safest to keep an eye on each other.

A good example was the day after the projectile fake Diet Coke incident. Hayden came out of his room after a post-work run—and yes, another shower—to find me on the couch reading a book on my e-reader as the sun set over the monuments and highways outside our window.

"Hey, do you mind if I put something on out here?"

I looked up at him in surprise. He'd never asked to share the living room like this before.

"Oh yeah, sure. Do you want me to move?"

"No, that's fine. It's a big sectional. I'd watch on my tablet in my room, except today is the premiere of the new *Star Wars* show, *Bounty Hunter Wars*, on Disney+, and it's really meant to be watched on a big screen, you know?"

"Oh yeah. I mean, no, I don't know. I've never seen any *Star Wars*, but I can understand that something with special effects like that would be better enjoyed on a bigger screen."

Hayden looked at me, dumbfounded.

"You've never seen *Star Wars*? Not even a single Star War? Not one movie?"

I laughed at his expression.

"No, we're a book family, remember? We didn't even have a TV until PBS started showing *Sherlock*. That was something we had to watch. And then it was just all too much to catch up on. I did get that *Arrested Development* reference, though."

"Well, at least there's hope for you yet."

Hayden settled himself on the couch, his wet hair tossed messily on his head, the ends curling slightly. After seeing him in mostly suits for the past few days, it was a little jarring to see him relaxed in joggers and a Henley, sitting on the couch with a beer. There was towel-wearing Hayden, high-powered suit Hayden, and then prankster Hayden, but I wasn't quite sure yet who this guy would be.

Hayden grabbed the remote and navigated to the app.

"So, what's the show about?"

"Well, the whole *Star Wars* universe would be considered a sci-fi western. This series features bounty hunters, all competing for one prize, but the prize isn't what it seems and starts to fight back."

"I understand most of those words individually, but in that order, you've completely lost me."

"It's set in space and has that hot guy in it that's all over all the magazines. You know, the one with the bear claw tattoo on his shoulder."

"Oh, Elias Roblés? Enough said. Cue it up!"

The opening sequence started to play, and I was immediately lost.

"So, wait, there are droids and then there are huma—"

Hayden pauses the show and looks at me the way one might look at a child who's just asked if we're there yet for the fiftieth time in an hour.

"I'm all for dissecting a show or movie, but not during the first viewing. Make notes on your phone with your questions. We'll watch it through once and then watch it again and talk the whole way through, okay?"

I felt myself smiling, despite his obvious impatiently calm tone.

"Okay, got it. My lips are sealed. To infinity and beyond."

Hayden heaved a heavy sigh, obviously regretting all the choices he had made in the last few minutes, but pressed play nonetheless.

I got into the show and the action, writing down some questions, but found myself watching Hayden just as much as the action on the screen. His eyes were wide with childlike wonder and he laughed at jokes that were obviously made for the in-crowd with such glee, I knew this franchise meant a lot to him.

After the show was over, I got up to get another round of drinks and made some popcorn before we started the rewatch.

"So, *Star Wars*, huh?" I asked from the kitchen, looking at the back of Hayden's head from where he sat on the short arm of the sectional.

"Yeah, the first prequel was the last movie we saw in theaters as a family, before my mom got sick. My parents loved the movies from their childhood and with a family of all boys, made us all fans too. My dad worked *a lot* while we were growing up to make sure we could all stay together, but always made sure he was around to take us to opening day of the second and third prequels. It's just... a family thing."

I didn't know what to say. I knew Margaret was their step-mom, and their family had moved to Holly Ridge after their dad married Margaret, but didn't know all the history. It's hard to tell a person's emotions from the back of their head, especially when you've only known them for a week, but the way Hayden brought his hand up to grasp the back of his neck, the skin around his fingertips turning red from the pressure, told me he was dying for a subject change.

I walked back toward the couch, the bowl of popcorn in one hand, my glass of wine in the other, and his bottle of beer wedged between my elbow and my chest. I stopped in front of him, awkwardly thrusting the neck of the bottle toward him, realizing too late that motion also thrust my cleavage in his face. Hayden slowly freed the bottle from its precarious grasp, his eyes trained somewhere between the glass neck and mine.

I cleared my throat as I nestled back into my corner of the couch, my feet pointing at his hip. "So."

He shook his head. "So. Any hints on what objects of mine around the house I should look out for tomorrow?"

"C'mon Brandt, you know I can't take it easy on you. You'll just have to be on your... toes," I smiled.

"You put something in my shoes again, didn't you, Charlotte?"

Something shivered down my spine at the way he said my name, all stern, yet anticipatory-like.

"Restart the show, Hayden. I've got questions that need answered."

CHAPTER
Nine

HAYDEN

The pranks with Charlotte had gotten a bit more personal since the night we watched the first episode of *Bounty Hunter Wars* on the couch.

Waking up to a picture of Jabba the Hutt taped to my mirror is not something I need to do again and took approximately three years off my life. I never considered myself a heavy sleeper, but Charlotte was like a ninja in the dark.

I might have ordered a used copy of the bodice ripper she was reading and replaced the pages with a Clone Wars novel, hiding her real copy. The talking to I got about the sanctity of destroying books for that one was equal parts hilarious, arousing, and a little terrifying.

I don't think either of us was actually trying to scare the other person away anymore, but were instead using the pranks as a shield to stop the other person from getting any closer. The way I had easily told her about *Star Wars* and the important role it played in my childhood... that was dangerous.

I was unpacking a mountain of Chinese food, the delivery driver left my order and another order by mistake, when Charlotte stormed in the door after 8:oo p.m. She had been working later and later as some gala she was working on got closer.

"Hey Charlotte, I've got extra Chinese if you want any."

The response I got was more scream than words.

"Sorry, can you try that again? I don't speak angry dolphin."

"Ha, ha," she responded, heading to the fridge to grab her wine but came back with a bottle of my IPA instead.

"She speaks! And sure thing, help yourself."

"Thanks. I just didn't think pinot grigio went especially well with kung pao chicken. And I could use something with a bit more of an edge tonight."

"Rough day at the office, schnookums?"

Charlotte rolled her eyes at me, a reaction I was growing to appreciate a little too much. She reached for a fork from the island drawer and a white container, not bothering with a plate, before scooping steaming chicken into her mouth.

"You could say that. Last night, all of a sudden, I started getting these text messages to my work phone from people asking if I still had a llama for sale. There's a lot of weirdly motivated people interested in buying llamas."

I went still, noodles dangling from the fork halfway to my mouth from my own carton of spicy goodness. *Oh fuck. The llama prank. That was her work phone?* Somehow, Charlotte and I had been living together for several weeks and hadn't yet exchanged phone numbers. The night after the mirror prank, I swiped the phone she left sitting on the counter one night when she was in the bathroom and sent myself a text before deleting it to get her number for a prank. I didn't even know she *had* a work phone. Let alone, that's the number I had gotten.

"The texts have just been pouring in nonstop, especially when I don't respond to them, and just keep on coming. Anyway, all the traffic got flagged by IT, wondering why I'm using my work phone for personal matters and it took me ten minutes to convince the guy I've never seen a llama in real life, let alone have one up for sale." When I didn't respond, Charlotte looked up from the Chinese container. I forced out a fake laugh, and she narrowed her eyes at me.

"Wait a minute... did you?"

I put the container down and put my hands up in defense.

"I had Hunter set it up almost two weeks ago. I had no idea that was your work number and not your personal number. I thought it would be funny? And also, it's a *llama* in the middle of a city. Who knew there would be such demand?"

"Oh my God, Hayden, what the *fuck*?" Charlotte slammed the chicken box onto the counter with such force it tipped over and bits of sauced chicken spilled all over the surface.

"Why would you think that's okay, even if it was my personal phone? Putting my number out there where anyone could find it? They were calling me by name. You're such a man, not even thinking about how dangerous that is for a woman."

"You're right. I never thought about that. I'm sorr—"

"And then there's the fact it's my *work* phone. This internship is one of the biggest opportunities I've ever gotten. If I don't get a job out of this, I have to go back home with my tail between my legs and just wait while my parents don't listen to me and the store goes out of business. Do you think that's what I want? Now I'm going to be known as the country llama lady who abuses company assets."

"I'm sure no one is thinking—"

"Ugh, I can't even look at you right now. I'm going to bed."

With that, Charlotte stormed away from the island, slamming her bedroom door behind her. She left the mostly full beer bottle and had only gotten through a few bites of dinner, which I knew wasn't going to help her anger toward me.

I pulled out my phone and dialed the number of my twin, Hunter.

"Hey, man," he answered.

"Hey, Hunter, listen. Can you do me a favor and take down that llama ad from wherever you posted it? And scrub it from appearing again?" I may be the professional IT guy in the family, but I had accidentally taught Hunter enough to be dangerous.

"Yeah, sure, no problem. Did she figure out it was you?"

"Yeah... I ended up telling her. Turns out that was her work number and not her personal one. And she read me the Riot Act about using her real name on the ad too."

"Wait, Charlotte's her real name? What the hell, man? Even *I* know not to put a woman's real name with her phone number on the internet."

"Well, I know now, don't I? Just get the ad down?"

"Consider it done."

"Thanks, man. Love you."

"You too."

I stared at the screen of my phone, wondering if there was anything else I could do to make it right. I could call someone at her job? But then she might get in trouble for leaving her phone around unlocked, where someone else could access it. Plus, who was I, her dad, trying to get her out of trouble?

I looked down the hall at the closed door, almost feeling Charlotte's rage radiating in waves on the air out toward me. Maybe I didn't want Charlotte to get any closer, but I sure didn't like the idea of her feeling this far away.

CHAPTER

Ten

CHARLOTTE

It had been two weeks since I was last contacted about selling a llama, but I was still strongly considering selling a Hayden. The leaves were starting to turn and pumpkin spice everything was everywhere. I had bought the dairy version of pumpkin spice creamer just in case Hayden liked to indulge in his basic side; he didn't deserve to sneak any into his morning coffee.

We hadn't talked much since his big prank reveal. I could tell he wanted to make it up to me in the days right after, but I hadn't given him much opportunity. Since that night, he stayed at the office later each day, barely spending any time in the condo. It turns out I hadn't needed to resort to pranks to get him out of the house, just wait for him to screw up on a monumental scale all on his own. Then he'd treat it as a place to rest his head and nothing more.

I did wonder though, where he had been watching episodes of *Bounty Hunter Wars*.

My hours weren't much better than Hayden's, with the gala getting closer every day. It seemed there were a million little details to take care of, from the flowers to the seating chart to the silent auction. I loved it and felt like I was thriving. Even better, it appeared Paula did, too. The "llama incident" seemed to be a distant memory at work, but I was still having trouble letting it go.

On Monday morning, a whole week before the gala, it felt like I hadn't gotten any rest over the weekend. I spent Saturday tweaking the seating arrangements, as the RSVP deadline passed on Friday. Sunday had brought marathon phone calls with Blaire and Austin, but I hadn't felt like doing much else other than hiding in my room and scrolling on my phone.

As the elevator opened on my floor, Miles, another intern in the bookstore relations department, was walking past with a cup of coffee.

"Morning, Charlotte! Good weekend?"

"It was all right. Not much to write home about. How about you?"

"It was great. I was able to achieve the sporting quadfecta. Since the baseball team is in the playoffs, I attended games from all four DC sports teams this weekend! Only two of the teams won, and I don't want to see hot dogs and light beer again for a month, but it was a great time. Say, are you okay?"

We had reached my desk during Miles's story, and I felt my stomach lurch at his mention of stadium food staples. I reached for my stomach, pressing a hand on it, willing it to calm down.

"What's that? Oh yeah, I'm fine."

"You sure? You look a little flushed."

I touched my hand to my cheek. It did feel a little warm.

"Must be the walk from the Metro in this weird mid-October heat wave we're having. All good here. Well, I better dive into it. The gala is only twelve days away."

Miles smiled and nodded.

"I'm really looking forward to it! I'm hoping to bring someone I met at the hockey game this weekend. We exchanged numbers and they're a big book person too. Fingers crossed they text me back!"

I held up my crossed fingers and smiled, and Miles finally turned around and walked away. The smile dropped from my face as I let my body drop into my chair. Putting my head in my hand, I gave myself an internal pep talk. *All right, Charlotte. You may feel like death, but the gala doesn't care. Pull it together!*

I pulled my laptop out of my bag and set it on my desk, opening the lid and bringing the screen to life. I entered my password, opened up my spreadsheet, and got to work.

For the rest of the day, it seemed I was putting out fires on all fronts. I spoke to the linen contractor, spending forty minutes convincing him that peach was not an adequate substitute for rose gold. Then I got to spend a grueling thirty-five minutes on the phone with the caterer. We went over each and every nutritional need on the guest list, even though it had all been detailed in a nice, color-coordinated spreadsheet—that we both referenced during the call. And now, finally, I was heading to Paula's office to sit in on a call with Nieto Pharmaceuticals, the biggest donor for the gala.

My stomach hadn't returned to its non-queasy level of normal after my conversation with Miles this morning, and a pounding headache appeared as the day went on. I knocked on Paula's door and she ushered me in, finishing a phone call moments before Mr. Jackson, the head of outreach at Nicto, planned to call us.

I sat in a chair in front of her desk, a comfortable grey armchair that welcomed you into its deep cushions like you were meant to stay awhile. I doodled on the notepad in front of me, wondering if I could sneak out of the office after this meeting. I'm sure I just needed a solid twelve hours of sleep and then I'd be fine.

"Charlotte?"

I looked up to see Paula looking at me with concern on her

face, which led me to believe that wasn't the first time she had said my name.

"Oh yes, sorry! Lost in thought about those flower arrangements we settled on last week. Ready to talk to Mr. Jackson?"

"Are you okay, Charlotte? You look pale."

For the sixteenth time today, I started to say "I'm fi—," but I was saved by the ringing phone.

"This is Paula Lapman," Paula answered, putting the phone on speaker straight away.

"Hi, Paula, this is Andrew Jackson from Nieto Pharmaceuticals. Thanks so much for taking my call."

"Happy to do so, Andrew. I've got Charlotte here with me, who I believe you've been communicating with over the past few weeks."

"Ah, yes. Hi, Charlotte. Hope you're well. I'll just dive right into what I wanted to talk about today. Nieto isn't going to be a sponsor of the Storybook Ball Gala next week, I'm afraid."

Paula's eyes met mine, going wide. She indicated with her hand that I should address Andrew directly.

"I'm so sorry, Mr. Jackson, I don't understand. When I spoke to you last week, you gave me your company's guest list for your two tables and told me the check was in the mail."

"Ah yes, well, Charlotte, things have changed since our conversation last week. I'm not at liberty to discuss specifics, but a stop has been put on all outgoing payments, operational and philanthropic, effective immediately. It doesn't seem like that stop is going to be lifted anytime soon."

"I see," Paula said, in a voice that made it very clear she did not see how this was happening in the slightest.

"So sorry to have to deliver this news, and so close to the event. Our employees also won't be attending the gala. A ban has also been put on all appearances by personnel in relation to company events."

A beat of silence passed while Paula and I stared, dumbfounded, at the phone, projecting this bad news all over an already terrible day.

"Well... I've got another few of these calls to make today, so I'll have to let you go. Good luck."

And with that, Mr. Jackson ended the call.

"What are we going to do, Paula?" I asked shakily. I always wanted to project confidence and a self-assured presence in front of my boss, but I was having trouble finding the strength to do so now.

"Well, it's not a great thing. But there are other companies in the city. I'll call around to some of my contacts."

I feel like I'm going to throw up. This is such terrible news. Oh wait, no, I'm actually *going to throw up.*

I launched myself out of my chair and made it to the wastebasket inside Paula's door just in time to empty the contents of my stomach in spectacular fashion.

Paula was there beside me in an instant, tissues in hand, yelling out the door for her assistant to grab me a bottle of water.

I wiped my mouth with the tissues, mortified at hurling in front of the woman who was quickly becoming my mentor.

"I know it's bad timing, but I think I need to go home."

"I think you're right. Are you going to be okay getting there? Maybe you should take a car instead of the Metro."

The thought of navigating the blocks to the station, only to crowd onto a train with hundreds of other commuters, sounded absolutely miserable.

"That sounds like a good idea. I'll just head back to my desk and request one. I'm sure with a good night's sleep, I'll be right as rain and be back here tomorrow. We can figure this all out?"

Paula nodded in a motherly fashion that made me miss my mom for the first time in a long time.

"Keep me posted on how you're feeling, Charlotte. We'll come up with something."

I nodded meekly, then I headed back to my desk, accepting

the bottle of water from Paula's assistant that she held out to me as far away from her body as possible. That was easy for Paula to say. She's already cemented her legacy at the IBA.

Taking a car home was a much better idea than the Metro, but I still felt like I might ruin my passenger rating with a repeat performance at any moment. Luckily, I made it to my building without anything else leaving my body—other than carbon dioxide and several muttered curse words—and dragged myself out of the backseat and onto the sidewalk.

The trip to the fifteenth floor had never seemed longer, and as I put my key in the lock, I was surprised to find it already open. I pushed open the door, taking a few slow steps in, and dropped my bag on top of the shoe rack in the entryway, too exhausted to carry it another foot.

The door-unlocker himself was in the kitchen and he turned around as he heard me enter. His guarded face morphed into one of concern as he took me in, but I was too miserable to respond. I took a few steps into the foyer—unsure if I was aiming for the couch, the bathroom, or my bed. I just knew I needed to no longer be standing.

The last thing I heard before everything went dark was a deep, concerned voice asking, "Charlotte, are you okay?"

CHAPTER
Eleven

HAYDEN

It was the first time I made it back to the apartment before dark in two weeks. Once I realized Charlotte was going to ice me out completely, it seemed much more attractive to put in ten- or twelve-hour days at the office. Our building's water was out for emergency repairs this afternoon though, so I found myself home in the daylight for once.

I was standing in the kitchen, wondering what to do with myself, when I heard the door open. I braced myself for Charlotte's cold shoulder as I heard her drop her bag in the entryway.

Turning around to face her, anything I considered saying to make her talk to me again abruptly left my brain when I took in her appearance. Charlotte's skin had taken on a grey pallor and she looked like she had run a marathon to get home. Her usually well-kept hair was plastered to her forehead with sweat.

"Charlotte, are you okay?"

No sooner had the words left my mouth, I saw Charlotte stumble forward and start to fall to the floor.

"Fuck!"

Flinging myself toward Charlotte's falling body and sliding along the hardwood of the entryway, I managed to get my hands under her head before it hit the hard surface of the floor. While I wished I had been closer to stop any part of her from aching tomorrow due to the contact, I was relieved we didn't have to add concussion to our list of current concerns.

She was burning up.

I gently laid her head on the floor so I could get into a crouching position, then I slid my hands under her shoulders and knees to lift her.

I slowly got into a standing position, careful to adjust my grip to ensure she was secure in my arms. Charlotte's head lolled so her face pressed into my bicep, and I realized this was the first time I had touched her on purpose. Sure, there were the times we ran into each other on those first days of being roommates, and normal "pass me the remote, I'll grab you a beer" contact had been made, but there had never been a situation where I intentionally reached out to hold her. Her weight in my arms felt grounding, and under a slightly sweet smell of sweat from her obvious fever was the scent of jasmine and vanilla.

Charlotte stirred, her nose rubbing against the starchy cotton of my button-down. Her eyes fluttered open and she jolted, almost dumping herself right back on the floor again.

"Shit, Hayden. What happened? Why am I in the air? *How* am I in the air?"

"Easy, Char. You fainted right after you got in the door. I'm going to get you to bed."

"Fuck. Well, put me down. I can walk."

Ignoring her request, I made my way down the hallway and paused for a second outside of her room. I had the strongest urge to put her in my bed, where I could easily keep an eye on her, but considering this was the most she had said to me in two weeks, she'd be more comfortable in her own room.

I shouldered Charlotte's door open and set her on the bed.

I took a step back, giving her some space, as she swung her legs so they dangled over the bed and put her head in her hands.

"Dumb question, but how are you feeling?"

"Like I got hit by a truck," she mumbled, not moving her head to respond.

"Well, that's probably a combo of the fever and the fall to the tile. I'm just glad I got there before your head hit the ground."

At that, Charlotte looked up at me.

"Oh. Well, thanks…"

Whatever she was going to say next was interrupted by her sudden rush out the door to the bathroom. The sounds of her retching reached me as I stood awkwardly in her room.

Should I wait here for her to come back? No, I'll go get her some supplies from the kitchen.

I walked down the hallway, pausing for a moment outside the bathroom door, but it sounded like this episode had calmed down. I filled a glass with water, grabbed some ibuprofen from the cupboard, and snagged the Liquid IV I stashed for after my runs out of the cupboard, mixing it with a cold bottle of water from the fridge. Then I grabbed a clean dish rag and ran it under the faucet, ringing the cold cloth out so it wouldn't drip all over the floor on my way back to Charlotte's room. As I gathered everything up, I heard the bathroom door open and the sound of feet shuffling on the carpet as Charlotte made her way back to her room. I followed quickly behind and almost ran into her back as she stopped, stock still, in the middle of her room.

"Char?"

"I can't decide if I need to throw up again, change out of these sweaty clothes, or just pass out for the rest of the day."

I eased my way to her left and set the supplies—save the wet towel—on top of her dresser.

"Why don't you get into bed, and I'll grab you something more comfortable. Do you want something to drink?"

As I said this, I reached for the top drawer of Charlotte's dresser. "No wait! Not that one!"

I put my hands in the air and turned around to find Charlotte leaning on the edge of her bed. An eyebrow rose as I took in Charlotte's pink cheeks, though that may have been the fever.

"So, what's in that one?"

She rolled her eyes at me, and I couldn't help my small smile. She may feel awful, but spunky Charlotte was still in there, and it was the first I had seen her in too long. This felt good.

"Just grab a T-shirt from the second drawer, please? The big green Holly Ridge Christmas Festival one?"

I turned back around and grabbed the shirt, noticing how the scent of jasmine and clean linen greeted me as I pulled the cloth out of its folded home. I tried to inhale as deeply as I could while maintaining subtlety and turned back to Charlotte, bringing the glass of water and the pills with me. The vanilla must come from her shampoo or body wash.

"Here you go. And, you should take these and try to drink as much of this as your stomach will allow. You're burning up. You should try to break the fever."

"Thanks," Charlotte said, taking the shirt and laying it in her lap and swallowing the pills and a small mouthful of water gingerly, seeming to not want to test her stomach's capacity for liquid.

I stared at her throat as she swallowed the water down, noticing how the long lines of her neck led to a swath of creamy skin exposed by her blouse's scoop neckline.

"Um, do you mind? I'd love to get out of these clothes..."

"Oh, uh, sure." I turned around, staring at the vent on the wall, starting to count the openings. Anything to avoid listening closely to the sound of cloth rubbing against Charlotte's skin as she worked her clothes off, the rustling of sheets while she tried to manage without getting up.

What the fuck, man? She's sick and probably still mad at you. You need to get laid.

"So, uh, what do you usually need when you're sick? I can run to the store or order something. Gatorade? Chicken noodle soup? Any particular medicine?"

"I'm fine. I'm just going to sleep it off. I'm sure this is just a twenty-four-hour bug. And after Nieto… anyway, I can't miss any more work this week."

Something in her voice made me risk a peek over my shoulder and seeing she was safely cocooned in her blankets, the oversized hunter green shirt coming down to expose one shoulder, I turned around. She looked so small there in her bed, and she sounded so defeated when talking about needing to get back to work. It made me want to stay and take care of her, but as her eyes dropped from mine, I knew I had been dismissed.

"Okay, well, I'll just be out on the couch catching up on emails. Just give me a shout if you need anything."

"I will."

I walked the short distance to the doorway.

"And Hayden?"

Charlotte's voice stopped me in the entryway and I looked back to see her laying on her side, blankets drawn up to her chin, eyes drooping.

"Yeah, Charlotte?"

"Thank you."

Again, I felt the urge to take care of her. Tuck that wayward blond strand behind her ear, rub her back, something.

"Anytime," I responded instead.

It turned out to be a very long night. Charlotte visited the bathroom several more times. Each time, I snuck into her room and refilled her water bottle. After the second trip, she stopped closing the door behind her. I took this as an invitation to replace her cold rag when she kicked all the blankets off—one of her trips had resulted in some short sleep shorts that I suppose in theory were more concealing than underwear—and then removed it and tuck the blankets around her chin when I peeked in and saw her shivering in her sleep. I got her to take a few more doses of medicine throughout the night, though it didn't seem to control the fever, and I was relieved to see dawn breaking through the windows of the living room from my vigil on the couch.

I heard Charlotte shuffling down the hall and assumed she was visiting the bathroom again, but heard the sound continue to the kitchen, where she proceeded to take a mug out of the cupboard.

"Hey there, sickie. Whatcha doing?" I asked, bounding from the couch and into the kitchen.

"Making some coffee. I need a zap of energy so I can shower and get ready to go into the office."

"Uh, coffee? Office? Charlotte, your stomach isn't keeping down water right now. I don't think—" She slammed the mug onto the counter, surprisingly, not cracking the ceramic with the force.

"Well, it's going to have to figure it out. I have to go to work today and figure out how we're going to replace ten thousand dollars from Nieto Pharmaceuticals, so the gala isn't a failure. So, I'm going to work, and you aren't going to stop me."

Charlotte moved to put water in the machine, the mug dropping out of her hand as her arm started to shake. This time, it did break, and she had to prop herself up on the counter to stay upright.

I was next to her in an instant, putting my arm around her to help hold her up, noticing her whole body was shaking now, with tears.

"Char, I know this job means a lot to you, but I really don't think you can go in. Can I help you get back to bed? I'll clean this up later."

She nodded and let me guide her away from the counter.

"On second thought, why don't you sit on the couch for a second? I'll strip your bed, change the sheets, and throw the dirty ones in the wash so we can do it again later if we need to, okay?"

Charlotte nodded again, and I sat her down on the couch and

tucked a blanket around her lap, noting tears were still streaming down her cheeks.

I think I earned a gold medal in bed changing that day. With Dad working as much as he did, Duncan had us divvy up the chores around the house, and laundry was one of mine. Five young and pre-teen boys dirtied a lot of sheets, and we didn't have extras, so I got pretty good at making beds over the years. I never thought I'd be thankful for all that laundry, but as I tucked Charlotte into clean sheets within five minutes of posing the idea, suddenly, I was.

"I need to call Paula and tell her I can't come in and just relay a few things I need someone to take care of. Where's my phone? Did you see my phone when you changed the sheets?"

"I didn't. Did you have it after you got home yesterday?"

"I have no idea. Maybe it's still in my bag?"

She started to get up, and I pushed her back down with a gentle hold on her shoulder.

"I'll go look. You stay here."

I started back for the living room, when my phone rang in my pocket. I had never been so glad to see Leslie's name in the weeks I'd known her.

"Morning, Leslie."

"Morning, Hayden. I saw your email when I got up this morning and put some feelers out. A Dr. Nguyen will be at your place at 9:30 to visit Charlotte. Does that sound okay?"

"That sounds amazing. Thank you so much, Leslie."

"How's she doing this morning?"

"Still the same. I just had to stop her from trying to go to work. I better get back to her before she starts trying to get dressed or something."

Leslie laughed.

"Sounds like a woman after my own heart. I'm glad I could help you take care of her. I assume you'll be working from home today?"

"Yeah, I think so, and maybe the rest of the week, too? I'll keep you posted. Let's check in this afternoon?"

"You got it. Have Dr. Nguyen send the bill to my email address, and I'll take care of that, too."

"You're a lifesaver, Leslie. Thanks again."

I hung up, thankful that a perk of living in a big city was having doctors that could make house calls with a few hours' notice.

I reached for Charlotte's bag, still where she had dropped it upon her entrance yesterday. Her phone was resting on top. The screen lit up with missed calls and notifications. Grabbing the phone and hanging the bag on the hook in the entryway, I was thinking about how I would need to stop her from returning all these calls when her phone vibrated in my hand.

The name Austin appeared on the screen, one I had seen several calls and texts from. Before I could stop myself, my thumb swiped across the bar and I answered the call.

"Hello, Charlotte's phone, Hayden speaking."

"Well, hello, Hayden. Is Charlotte available? Or did you accidentally murder her in another prank gone wrong?"

"Charlotte can't come to the phone right now. I'll let her know you called."

I pulled the phone away from my ear, moving to hang up the call, when I heard a tinny voice from the speaker shout, "Wait, wait!"

I put the phone back to my ear.

"Yes?"

"Look, I'm just worried about her. She mentioned she got sick at work yesterday when she was on her way home and then she didn't answer any of my texts or calls. Seriously, is she okay?"

"Would she be comfortable with me sharing this information with you? What's your relationship?"

The man apparently known as Austin laughed in my ear.

"Subtle, man. I'm Austin, one of her best friends from back

home. You don't have to tell me colors or smells, just that she's okay."

Best *friend*, huh? Not a boyfriend or love interest then. *Interesting.*

"She's okay. It was a rough night, but a doctor will be here to take a look at her in an hour. She just needs fluids and rest, I think. I hope. Do you know what she likes when she's sick? Like a type of sports drink or a certain brand of crackers? I want to get the right stuff."

There was silence from the other end of the line before Austin continued. "Hayden, what's *your* relationship with Charlotte?"

"All right, well, if you're done being helpful…"

Austin laughed.

"Okay, okay, I get it. She likes blue Gatorade the best and prefers saltless Saltines. I'll never know why. Thank you for looking after her. Can you have her text me later today, just to check in?"

"As long as she's feeling up to it, I'll pass along the message."

"Strict, aren't you? I think Charlotte needs that. Well, maybe I'll talk to you again sometime soon then. Bye, Hayden."

And at that, the line went dead.

Phone in hand, I walked back to her room, already gone longer than I had planned.

Charlotte was reclining against her pillows, eyes closed. I hated to disturb her, but I knew she'd want to call her boss.

"Hey. Here's your phone."

I handed it to her as her eyes opened.

"Oh, thanks. Who were you talking to out there?"

Busted.

"Austin called your phone, it… accidentally got answered while I was taking it out of your bag. He was worried, so I let him know you were okay, and that you'd reach out later if you felt up to it. It looked like there might have been a lot of worried people on there, but take it easy with the outside contact. You need to rest."

Charlotte nodded.

"I need to call Paula, and I think that might take a lot out of me. I feel so bad leaving her in a lurch on *my* project when we really need to replace all that money..."

"You rested and well will be more help than you would be today."

She nodded. "You're right. Okay, well, I better make this call."

That was my cue.

"I'm going to go order some supplies. A doctor will be here to examine you in a little over an hour. I wasn't sure you'd be up for leaving the house."

Her eyes flew to mine. "You didn't need to do that."

"I know. Make your call."

And with that, I headed to the kitchen to give her some privacy, putting in a delivery order for all manner of blue Gatorades and saltless crackers, as well as sending a text to Leslie to get me contact information for Charlotte's boss. I may not have earned that full charitable committee duty yet, but that doesn't mean I didn't have influence with the big boss and how we directed our funds. I might be able to make one of Charlotte's worries disappear.

And I won't spend too much time dwelling on why I cared so much.

CHAPTER
Twelve

CHARLOTTE

I wasn't good at being sick on a normal day, but when I felt like my future at the IBA hung in the balance, it was especially difficult to have my body disobey me.

Paula was incredibly understanding when I got her on the phone. She forbade me from sending a follow-up email detailing the to-do items I relayed to her and told me she wouldn't be answering any calls from me to check in until tomorrow. I wasn't used to care and concern for my well-being from a role model. I once had to work at the bookstore with a 102-degree fever—pre-pandemic, of course—because my parents couldn't find any coverage and they were away at a trade show. The store being closed instead just wasn't an option in their eyes.

I was dozing lightly after my phone call when I heard a knock at my door.

"Charlotte? Dr. Nguyen is here. If you're ready to see him?"

I pushed myself up in the bed so my back was against the headboards. "Yeah, sure, send him on in."

Hayden moved aside so a kindly older man with greying hair, wire glasses, and kind eyes could walk into the room.

"Hi there, Charlotte. Hayden let me know you had a bit of a rough twenty-four hours or so."

Hayden settled in against the doorjamb, apparently not content to let me or the doctor out of his sight. I knew I could ask him to leave, HIPAA and all, but given how out of it I felt from the fever and lack of nutrition, it was probably good someone else was here to supervise.

"You can say that again. If upchucking was an Olympic event, I'd be on the medal stand for sure."

Dr. Nguyen laughed gently behind his mask.

"Well, let's see what we can do to get you feeling better. First things first, let's do a few rapid tests to see what we can rule out. While we're waiting for those results, I'll start an IV and get some fluids in you." He pinched my skin gently and watched how slow it was to return to its normal state. "Hydration is the name of the game."

He looked at Hayden. "I'm assuming Charlotte consents to you being here, but you should put on a mask for the time being, just in case."

Hayden pulled a mask out of the pocket of his joggers like he was prepared for this inevitability and didn't want to leave my side for a moment.

Dr. Nguyen swabbed my nose for each test and mixed the solutions. While we waited the fifteen minutes for the results to appear, he started an IV in my arm—as promised—hanging the bag off my headboard.

That's a new headboard accessory I never thought I'd see, I thought to myself, holding back a giggle. The fever must be getting to me, bringing out those types of thoughts in front of the kind, if grandfatherly, doctor.

Dr. Nguyen measured my pulse and oxygen rate, and the timer went off. He examined the test strips. "The flu test came back positive. Everything else came back negative, which I can imagine is a relief."

I nodded. "Of course. I have a big event at work next week,

so being out for a long period is just out of the question at the moment."

Dr. Nguyen's eyes turned stern. "You're still a pretty sick young lady. The flu is nothing to scoff at. Hayden let me know that your fever wasn't especially responsive to ibuprofen, which to me means bed rest for at least three days. I'll leave you with some other prescriptions to help control the fever and stop this from turning into something more serious, like pneumonia, but pushing yourself back to work too soon is a sure way to help yourself along that path."

"But, no, I really need to be back in the off—"

"Don't worry, Doc. I've cleared my schedule to work from home for the rest of the week. I'll be sure to keep her home and in bed," Hayden interrupted from his vigil in the doorway.

A shiver worked its way through my body at the thought of Hayden keeping me in bed. Glad I could blame the fever if anyone questioned me on it.

"That's going to be for the best. I'll leave you both with my card if things get worse, but I expect with lots of rest, fluids, and medicine, you'll be in good shape. I can send one of my nurses by with another fluid IV tomorrow if you need it. Just call the office."

I slumped in my bed, my arms crossed. Logically, I knew I needed the rest, but I'd always been stubborn and didn't appreciate these two *men* telling me what to do.

Dr. Nguyen got up and packed up his bag, trying to hide the grin that reached his eyes and failing to do so when he needed me to uncross my arms so he could remove the IV from its place in my arm.

"You've got a good man here, Charlotte."

I opened my mouth to tell Dr. Nguyen exactly what I thought about the man sharing this condo with me—that he was overbearing, and sure, a hot-as-hell control freak—but Hayden beat me to responding. He crossed the room, his hand extended. "Thanks so much again for coming by Dr. Nguyen."

Hayden and the doctor left the room, and I heard them continuing to talk in low tones as Hayden presumably walked him toward the door. I maneuvered myself into a horizontal position. I felt better with the additional fluids in my system, but somehow, I was still exhausted from the events of the morning, even though it felt like I'd done nothing but sleep—and throw up—for the last eighteen hours.

Hayden returned to the room, not bothering to knock since I was lying on my side facing the door and saw him coming.

"Here," he said, placing a Gatorade and a sleeve of crackers on my nightstand.

I picked my head up slightly.

"How did you know blue was my favorite?"

"I, uh, may have checked with Austin when we talked earlier. The crackers are unsalted too."

I felt a warmth in my stomach that had nothing to do with any nausea I felt at that moment. It didn't surprise me at all that Austin knew what I'd want. Our friendship wasn't that old, but the guy had a freaky good memory and we had talked about childhood sickness cures when he was sick last year. I was touched that Hayden had thought to ask him, though. What's more, he had gone through all the trouble of arranging a house call from a doctor and clearing his schedule to keep an eye on me.

"If you're not careful, you're going to find yourself forgiven for the whole llama-text debacle, Hayden Brandt," I said as my eyes closed, feeling myself drifting off to sleep, unable to stay awake any longer.

As I faded toward unconsciousness, I detected the ceiling light in my room switching off, and thought I heard Hayden whisper, "That's what I'm counting on," before blackness took me.

Τ he rest of the day was still miserable. The first Gatorade did not stay down, but after some time and a nausea pill, I kept the second one down, along with some crackers. This gave me strength enough to take a quick shower, after which I returned to clean sheets, still warm from the dryer. And again, I found external factors like a toasty bed had little to do with the warmth spreading through my insides.

The next day, it had been almost twenty-four hours since I'd last thrown up. I followed Paula's instructions and had not called the office again yesterday, but I was itching to hear from her after I called and reached her assistant this morning.

Like my thoughts had summoned her, my phone rang at that moment.

"This is Charlotte."

"Hi Charlotte. Your voice sounds stronger today. How are you?"

"I'm feeling a lot better. Maybe I'll actually allow the sun to hit my face from the balcony a little later today. Things might get wild. How are you? How are things with the gala?"

"Well, I'm only returning your call because I thought you might keep calling if I didn't, and because I have good news to share. We found a donor to replace Nieto Pharmaceutical's pledge and then some. We're going to be able to get flowers for every table now, not just the decorative arrangements we had originally planned."

I shot up into a seated position

"What? That's *amazing*. Who's the donor? How did we find them?"

"The donor requested to stay anonymous until the night of the event. Now, I'm going to let you go so you can get back to resting, and we can get back to working through your incredibly detailed and thorough checklist. Rest well, Charlotte. Everything is going to be okay. We'll see you back here at the beginning of next week."

"But the doctor sai—"

"Beginning of next week, Charlotte. You can't pour from an empty cup. We'll see you then."

I looked at my phone in disbelief. Where had another donor come from? Honestly, I didn't even care. I was just relieved the gala was saved. I was a little disappointed I hadn't had a role in securing it, but the relief was a hell of a lot stronger.

A knock came at the door.

"How are you feeling, Charlotte?"

Hayden stood in the doorway, appearing freshly showered, the scent of his body wash wafting into the room from where he stood, drawing up visions of a green, lush forest, a far cry from a gross and confined sick bed. He ran a hand through the still-wet ends of his hair. The grey joggers slung low on his hips, along with the tight white T-shirt, should be illegal. The guy made working from home look *good*.

"I'm feeling better, I think. Though that might be the endorphins. Paula just called. We found another donor for the gala, somehow, somewhere. She doesn't want me back until the beginning of next week now, which will be hard, but they found my checklist and that's a huge worry lifted, so I suppose I'll survive."

Something flickered across Hayden's face that I couldn't identify before he broke into a grin.

"That's great news, Char. And how's the nausea and fever?"

"Still vomit and hallucination-free over here."

Hayden laughed softly.

"Glad to hear it. Think you might be up for some chicken soup? I can run down to the deli on the corner and grab some."

"Sure, why not? Let's live a little. I might even move to the couch to eat it."

Hayden held up his hands.

"Now, now, let's not push it. I got a tray so you can eat in here. We'll leave couch excursions for tomorrow."

I rolled my eyes. "Yes, sir. Whatever you say."

Hayden's eyes darkened slightly, but he shook his head and the moment was gone.

"I'll be right back with the soup. Or do you need to get up and use the facilities before I run out? Don't want to come back to you passed out on the floor again."

"I think I'll be okay."

Hayden's face turned serious.

"I saw you faint already once this week, Charlotte. That was enough."

His tone let me know he would not budge on this one.

"I'm okay. Really. I can wait until you get back."

Hayden's eyes narrowed.

"I promise I'll stay right here. Maybe I'll give Austin a call, give him proof of life."

Hayden nodded. "I'll be back before you know it, soup in hand."

He turned around, getting ready to head toward the door and the deli in question, when I said, "Maybe you can get yourself some and eat it in here with me? Let me know what I missed on *Bounty Hunter Wars* the past few weeks?"

Hayden stopped and looked over his shoulder at me.

"Explaining things to you before you watch them may or may not be worse than your interruptions during a live viewing. But I'm game to give it a try."

He turned back around and continued his quest to bring me soup. I looked down at my hands, feeling that warm feeling again, glad Hayden had walked away before the large smile broke across my face.

CHAPTER
Thirteen

HAYDEN

The next Monday, I convinced Charlotte I should take her to work via my car service, so she wouldn't tire herself out on her first morning back.

"So, this is how you get to work every morning?" Charlotte asked, sliding into the car ahead of me and scooting over to the far side.

"Duncan wanted to be sure his regular driver wasn't without work while he was away for such a significant time, so he left the contract open for me. Though I'll admit, not having to fight the masses every morning and afternoon isn't the worst thing."

"Yeah, who would want to mingle with the commoners on the Metro?" Charlotte teased, her cheeks pink with health and her eyes sparkling. It was so good to see her feeling better.

As the driver pulled into traffic from the front of our building, I started scrolling through my phone out of habit. Charlotte cleared her throat next to me.

"Are you sure it's not a big deal for you to drop me off? I don't want to make you late after keeping you home all week."

I put my phone face down on my lap and looked over at her.

"Not that it matters, because I'd send you in the car by yourself if I really needed to, but it turns out your office is only a few minutes from mine. It's not a problem at all."

Charlotte settled back into her seat, seeming pleased.

"Well, in that case, maybe I should be mad I haven't been getting this option all along. It's not like I stuffed paper towels in your shoe or anything. A girl could get used to this."

I laughed, turning my head away, hoping she couldn't see all over my face just how much I wouldn't mind sharing an enclosed space with her every weekday morning.

Being back in the office felt strange after almost a week of working from home. My suit felt weird and constricting on my body. I hadn't missed the way Charlotte took me in as I waited for her by the front door so we could head down in the elevator together.

As I rode the elevator to my floor, I thought back to our weekend. I got work done during her naps but gave myself completely over to a lazy weekend once five o'clock on Friday rolled around. We alternated movie picks and ordered in all weekend. I got Charlotte through the original trilogy of *Star Wars*, and I also secretly enjoyed Charlotte's picks: *Pitch Perfect*, *John Tucker Must Die*, and the adaptation of one of her favorite romance novels, *Red, White & Royal Blue*. Charlotte fell asleep watching football both Saturday and Sunday night. On Saturday, I tucked a blanket around her and tried to continue watching the game, only to wake up alone on the couch in the early hours of Sunday morning. Last night, I shook her awake, wanting her to get a good night's sleep before the start of a long week.

I checked my phone for a message from her, even though I had dropped her off just moments ago, only to be disappointed when there was nothing. There was no good excuse to keep us both in the apartment any longer, but I was still worried about her overdoing it on her first day back. The gala was Friday night, and I knew she was eager to dive back in and catch up. I knew re-energized was a feeling I should try to stir up in myself, but I was having trouble getting motivated. Instead, I found myself missing the Charlotte and Hayden clubhouse we had created.

I reached my office and was unsurprised to find Leslie already at her desk.

"Morning, Leslie," I greeted her, setting a cup of coffee on her desk. I asked my driver to stop so I could grab it for her after we dropped off Charlotte.

"Good morning, Mr. Brandt. What's this for? Usually, I'm the one getting coffee. You're depriving me of a trip to the gossip mines this morning."

I laughed.

"Feel free to go get a water or something else instead. I just wanted to thank you for all your help to set up the doctor for Charlotte and all the gatekeeping you must have done to allow me to have such a quiet week working from home. This afternoon's coffee run is yours as usual though, I promise."

"It was my pleasure. It was very chivalrous of you to drop everything and take care of your 'nuisance of a roommate' I believe is what I heard you call her to Preston not that long ago?" Her kind smile turned smug. Her tone told me she could see right through me.

"What can I say, us Brandt boys were raised right," I deflected.

Leslie shook her head, but thankfully let the subject drop.

"Speaking of Brandt boys, Duncan would like a video call before your 9:00 a.m. It's the only time he has today."

"No rest for the dutiful and chivalrous, I suppose," I said, walking to my office and opening the door. "I'll see you after my first meeting then, hopefully no later than ten-thirty."

"You're meeting with Ferguson and Mathes from IT, and you're the Chief Information Officer who disappeared from the building for four days. There's no chance I'm seeing you before eleven," came her response, accompanied by the clicking of keys, as Leslie returned to her work. She didn't even acknowledge my groan as I entered my office, shutting the door behind me.

I got settled quickly at my desk and pulled up our video conferencing software, hitting my brother's name from my contact list. The program rang once before the call connected and Duncan's face appeared on the screen.

"Hey, Dunc. Where in the European world are you today?" I asked, smiling at seeing my brother's face. It seemed we had communicated mostly through texts and emails since I started at Brandt Investing International just over two months ago, and while him being away allowed for my current living arrangements, I missed the guy.

"Today's the first of three days in Paris. This background isn't fake, you know."

I looked away from his face and noticed the blue sky with the black metal of the Eiffel Tower rising behind him. Scoffing, I rolled my eyes good-naturedly. "Show-off."

Duncan shrugged, which after thirty-one years of brotherhood, let me know he had, in fact, moved out onto the balcony to take my call. The noise from the street would bother him in any other scenario in which he wasn't showing off to one of his brothers.

"And what about your background, Hayden? Pray tell, are you actually in the office? Wave your arm behind you, so I can know that isn't a green screen set up."

I did, making sure my middle finger was the only one pointing up on my left hand as I waved it behind my head.

"Fuck you. So I worked from home unexpectedly last week. The report on the Polanski merger got submitted ahead of schedule, and I'm suffering through a meeting with both Ferguson and Mathes as soon as we hang up since I canceled on them both last week. I'm paying my price."

Duncan laughed. "Yeah, if they're in the room together, you'll be there for at least two hours, half of which will be them arguing with each other. I suppose that's as good a punishment as any I could dole out. So, everything's all good on the home front?"

I nodded. "Charlotte's feeling a lot better. She headed back to work today too, so I knew my time sloughing off was over."

"And should I make any comments about how you rearranged your entire work calendar to stay home and play nurse to a woman you once called 'a walking nuisance of white wine and bubbly energy'?"

Remind me to never introduce Charlotte to any of my brothers—ever.

"Nope, I don't think anything needs to be said."

"Okay, well, how about telling me about the large donation the company made to the"—Duncan glanced down at this tablet—"Independent Book Alliance's Bookstore Future Fund's Storybook Ball Gala? Want to tell me anything about that? Including why they couldn't name it something snappier?"

I paused, wondering how I should play this.

"You had threatened me with charity committee duty not that long ago, so I figured they might need a little direction. Their budget has a surplus compared to donations from last year, so I thought it was a good cause. You know Margaret loves Ridge Reads. She would be supportive."

Duncan stared at me for a moment, and I started to sweat, even though he was thousands of miles away from me.

"Yes, Margaret does love Ridge Reeds. Ridge Reads, owned by the Reid family—mother, Lillian; father, Jackson; and daughter, Charlotte. The same Charlotte who's working for the Independent Book Alliance this fall, living with you in my condo."

"What? Did you run a background check on her?"

Duncan smiled like a cat with a canary.

"Turns out, Bethany didn't leave any details of her arranging for Charlotte to stay in the place. She did, however, manage to run a background check and leave it in a file she opened when they first worked out all the arrangements. Once you texted about Charlotte being in the condo when you moved in, I reviewed it myself. Margaret may have made the arrangements for her to stay at my place, but she's a shrewd businesswoman. I knew she'd understand if the background check returned anything suspicious or iffy before I let her keep the keys to my DC kingdom."

I caved.

"Okay, fine. Charlotte's working directly for the fund during her internship, and they had a huge donor pull out of the gala last week, the day she got sick. I do think it's a good cause, but I also knew that if the donor money was replaced, she'd be more likely to stay home and rest, instead of throwing herself back into work too soon trying to find a way to replace it. The longer she was sick, the more likely it was I would have gotten sick, so really, I was just looking out for myself."

Duncan laughed, shaking his head, which told me exactly how much he bought that narrative.

"So, what did she say when you told her you took care of the funding problem?"

I sat in silence.

"You *did* tell her, right? Shit. Why didn't you tell her?"

I ran my hand through my hair, thankful that messy bedhead was always in style.

"She was kinda delirious with fever the day I made the call. And then that gave me too much time to think. I may have accidentally gone too far with a prank that interfered with her work and I was worried she wouldn't take too kindly to me involving myself with her job again in this way."

"Oh yes, because women notoriously hate it when men pony up tens of thousands of dollars to support a cause they believe in."

It was my turn to roll my eyes.

"Shut up, okay. I get it. I asked her boss to keep the donation anonymous until the gala on Friday night. She basically insisted they give us a table at the gala, given everything, so I'll be there and can tell her then. Or afterward. Or next week. It'll all come out sometime."

Duncan shook his head, pulling out his phone.

"I'm having my assistant email Leslie right now to put me on your calendar for next Monday morning. I need to know how you showing up unannounced to the gala, organized by your unwelcome surprise roommate-turned-patient-turned-whatever this is, works out for you. If she kills you, we'll just reschedule."

I put my forehead on my desk for a moment. The sound of Duncan's continued laughter in the background.

Sitting back up, I looked at my watch.

"Oh, would you look at the time? My 9:00 am will be here any minute, and I wouldn't want to keep them waiting."

Duncan settled himself. "At least not if you want to have lunch at a decent hour. But seriously, I think the IBA is a great cause and I'm glad you've gotten them into our philanthropy's rotation. I like it, and you're not wrong. Margaret will be pleased. You'll have to tell her at Thanksgiving. Or who knows, at this rate, Charlotte might be there, and can tell Margaret herself."

I hung up the call without saying goodbye to the sound of Duncan laughing at his own joke, casually sitting on a balcony with the Paris skyline in the background.

Brothers. You can't live with them, and certainly would have a stronger ego without them.

CHAPTER
Fourteen

CHARLOTTE

The week passed by in a blur. Thanks to our mysterious donor, and my love of a good spreadsheet, things weren't behind too much by the time I got back to work. Everything continued to sail smoothly through the rest of the week. Almost alarmingly smooth, if I'm being honest, but I suppose losing a donor and then expelling your weight in water over the course of two days is bad enough luck.

We were hosting the gala at the Washington Hotel, with plentiful views of the White House and the Washington Monument from the rooftop bar outside of the ballroom rented for the event. A member of the IBA board was part owner of the hotel, or else we could could never afford such a space while raising any money for the fund. I wasn't sure I would ever attend such a fancy and formal event again.

Rent the Runway came through with an amazing dress for the night, a silky, dark, ruby-red floor-length dress that played up my creamy complexion and light hair. I had enough time to shower and blow out my hair between setup and the start of the event. Of course, I was just a wall decoration to a lot of these guests, but I didn't want to stick out for being underdressed or under-coiffed.

Paula approached me, her arm tucked into the arm of a tall, gorgeous black woman around her age, both of them dressed in sparkly jewel-toned evening gowns.

"Charlotte, everything looks just wonderful. The best the gala has ever looked, in my opinion."

"I think so too," the woman on her arm agreed.

Paula smiled at her companion and turned her head back to me.

"Charlotte, I don't think you've had a chance to meet my wife, Valerie. Valerie, this is the Charlotte you've heard me praising over the past several weeks."

My cheeks warmed at the compliment.

"Valerie, it's so nice to have a chance to meet you. I'm glad you and Paula can make a date night out of tonight."

"Paula's firmly in work mode, but I'm here to have fun," Valerie replied, taking a sip of the champagne flute in her hand, her eyes sparkling.

"I'm sure she'll get me out there on the dance floor soon enough. It's okay to mix business and pleasure on certain occasions," Paula said, planting a kiss on her wife's cheek.

"Is there anything else you need? I've got the run of show for the event, so I'm ready to address the group after everyone's done eating," she asked, returning her eyes to mine after sharing a smile with Valerie.

I shook my head. "I think we're all set. I'm going to check in with the kitchen to be sure everything's set and on schedule for dinner service. It'll be time for me to welcome everyone before long."

"Well then, let's go check out the silent auction items, dear. Maybe you can win me a trip to Rome this year," Valerie said, gently pulling Paula in the direction of the tables in the back corner.

"Have fun," I called after them as they left.

I headed into the kitchen and confirmed with the caterer everything was on track, snagging a stuffed mushroom cap off a waiting tray on my way back to the room. All that time behind the cash register at Ridge Reads left me comfortable in these sorts of scenarios. I could make small talk with a tree if I needed to. I met many of DC's elite, who considered the IBA to be a priority for them. There were even a few members of Congress and their staff present.

Soon it was time to get dinner started, and I walked onto the stage, asking everyone to take their seats. The hum of the crowd grew to a loud buzz as our guests found their way to their tables for the evening. I had the seating chart memorized at this point, and my gaze wandered over to table fourteen, which had been reserved for our whiteknight, anonymous donors. I needed to eye the table to determine who I needed to thank for saving my ass.

A man approached the table who I had seen chatting with some of our politically related attendees earlier. He looked vaguely familiar, but I couldn't place where I knew him from. He shook hands with the man and woman already seated at the table and stood behind his chair, looking around expectantly, obviously waiting for someone. I checked my watch, noting we were right on schedule, and gazed back into the crowd to see if everyone was seated yet. My eyes came back to the familiar-looking man, his hand raised in a wave as he greeted his companion. My mouth dropped open in shock as Hayden stepped up to grab his extended hand, pulled him into a hug and patted the stranger on the back. They both turned to take their seats, and when I took in their faces side by side, I realized this must be one of Hayden's brothers. Otherwise, he had a knack for finding doppelgängers to be his friends. Hayden seemed to feel my gaze, as his eyes met mine and he raised his hand in a wave.

My eyes dropped to my notes, my mind racing. Hayden was

our mysterious donor? Well, I presume his brother's company was. It had been a corporate donation, but it seemed obvious Hayden was the driving force behind their support. The donation had come in after I had gotten sick and shared with him why I was so desperate to go to the office. *White knight, indeed.*

I shook my head slightly, not wanting Hayden's sudden appearance to throw me off task. It was time to get this shindig started off right.

"Hi everyone, and thank you so much for your support of the Independent Bookstore Alliance's Bookstore Future Fund. We dialed up some of the finest October weather here in the nation's capital tonight, so make sure you take advantage of the views from our vantage point on the top floor. We'll have dancing after dinner, and the silent auction bidding will close at nine thirty sharp, so be sure to stop by and bid generously on these amazing prizes. With no further ado, dinner is served."

Like clockwork, waiters appeared from the wings, carrying salads on trays. I felt a smile cross my lips. The gala was officially off and running. Mom resisted so many of my ideas for the store, but here, my ideas were not only listened to but implemented. It was a good feeling.

I maneuvered my way down the stairs leading from the stage, heading toward my chair at Paula's table to attempt to scarf down some food before my attention was inevitably needed elsewhere. I sensed Hayden's eyes following my path, but I absolutely needed food before I dealt with *that.*

I joined my coworkers and received their congratulations and warm wishes on the gala. It was hard not to hope they weren't jinxing me. There was a lot of evening left, but things should be mostly smooth sailing from here. I tried to pace myself on the salad waiting at my seat, but I realized I hadn't eaten anything since breakfast, and getting some calories in my system was an immediate necessity.

The salads cleared and waiters brought around bottles of

wine, looking to refill glasses. I held my glass up for the one glass of white I was allowing myself this evening and smiled at the young woman as she twisted the bottle expertly, not spilling a single drop.

"So, Charlotte, Paula tells me your family owns an independent bookstore in New England?"

I swallowed my mouthful of wine quickly and smiled at the older gentleman to my left.

"Yes, that's correct. It's a general interest bookstore in Holly Ridge."

A woman, who I assumed was the man's wife, leaned over, joining the conversation. "Al, I've told you about Holly Ridge. They're the town that hosts that lovely Christmas festival every year. I saw it on that blog about small-town festivals."

"We cohost the holiday festival with our neighboring town now. My best friend is the festival planner. It's a wonderful tradition. It'll be strange not being there in the lead-up this year, but I do like my work here."

The man I now knew as Al nodded. "It sounds like a lovely place with lots of history. Does your family's store do well there?"

I took a sip of wine, looking in Paula's direction to see if she was paying attention, hoping for a hint as to exactly who Al and his wife were and how candid I should be. Our dinner had just arrived at our table, so she was distracted tucking in, as well as continuing her conversation with her guests on her other side.

"We definitely have a rich history as the only general interest independent bookstore in the county. Like all stores, we struggle to compete with Jeff's website and other retailers who can offer books for less. It's part of why I'm so excited to have the chance to intern with the IBA. I think the work we do is important for stores like my family's."

Al's wife continued to lean in. "How did you all fare during the pandemic?"

I felt my cheeks start to warm. "It was a struggle. We didn't have an online ordering system, and what we have for non-in-person ordering isn't the most... ideal situation for the long-term. I'm not faking my enthusiasm for the Bookstore Future Fund. A lot of stores, Ridge Reads included, wouldn't have survived without it. But we have great support from our local community. It's just where we decide to go next that's up in the air."

Al's wife smiled kindly. "Your family must be missing you greatly while you're here. I can tell you're so passionate about the work of independent bookstores."

They miss my shift coverage, that's for sure.

I took a beat to cut my chicken while I considered my answer.

"I'm hoping what I've learned here will benefit Ridge Reads and many other bookstores in the future. We'll see where things lead me in December when my internship is up."

Al and his wife seemed satisfied with that and turned to interrogate the people on their other side.

I stabbed my fork into the potatoes on my plate, and while chewing, I saw Paula look at me and nod approvingly. It appeared I handled the inquisition well from her perspective.

I ate the rest of my food as quickly as was polite. More time had passed while I talked to Al and his wife than I realized. It was past time to check on the band, auction, and everything else that needed my attention.

I moved around the room, knowing that time for ignoring Hayden was drawing to an end. I had forgiven Hayden for the llama prank. I can't pretend his caretaking hadn't more than made up for it. That said, we had barely seen each other this week with me being up to my ears in gala planning. It also wasn't entirely clear why he hadn't told me he was the donor. Why the big reveal?

The bar on the far side of the room called to me. *Half a glass of wine more couldn't hurt, right? I'll call it the Hayden tax.* I smiled at the bartender as I approached. "Half a glass of sauvignon blanc, please," I said, as he placed a napkin in front of me. I picked the navy-blue paper up, twirling it in my hands while I waited for my wine. I felt his presence on my left side before I smelled his familiar cologne.

"Hi, Charlotte, fancy meeting you here."

CHAPTER
Fifteen

HAYDEN

"Are you just going to stare at her all night, or are you actually going to go talk to her?" Preston ribbed from his seat next to me.

"It's called choosing your moment, Prez. C'mon, is there no romance in your life?"

"Oh, so you want romance with Charlotte now, huh?"

Shit.

"Friendship can have moments too. So can roommates."

"Uh-huh, sure. Smooth."

"Why do you think she hasn't come over here to say hi to me yet? I mean, I, well, Brandt Investing International, did help save the gala after all." I could hear the uncertainty in my voice, taking a sip of my drink to try to settle my nerves.

"Probably because you're giving off really humble energy right now. And besides, I may not know romance, but I do know that women don't necessarily love it when you show up unannounced as a secret donor at their major important galas."

"You've been talking to Duncan, haven't you?"

Preston snickered into his drink.

I looked back at Charlotte's table and noticed she wasn't there anymore. With slightly more flailing than what could be considered cool and collected, I turned my head every which way, trying to find her. I knew Preston's razzing was in part to get me out of my head. But I had imagined a million ways tonight could go, but none of them had involved her avoiding me this long.

"She's over by the silent auction. Want to go flash more of your money around?"

"Last time I bring you as a date to anything, Preston, I swear to God."

Preston took another drink of his old-fashioned, presumably to smother another laugh. Smart move. I wasn't above making up a story to security to get him kicked out in front of all his colleagues from Congress.

"Okay, but seriously, Hayden, what's your move?"

"I'm just waiting for a chance to talk to her one-on-one, and we'll take it from there."

"Winging it—that's worked always in the history of ever."

"Writes speeches for a senator, don't you, Prez? I can see how with that sort of logic."

"Fuck you, these drinks are strong and dinner is still settling. Also, you're missing your moment yelling at me."

I followed Preston's gaze to the bar set in the far corner of the room and saw Charlotte standing there, presumably waiting for a drink.

"Well, brother, opportunity knocks."

"Go get 'em, tiger."

I rolled my eyes, but with that send-off I stood up from the table, buttoned my tux jacket, and made my way over to Charlotte. I found myself wanting it to be okay I was here, that I had intervened. Perhaps even have her happy to see me outside our shared walls.

I felt Charlotte's energy change as I stepped up to her side. Could she sense when I was near, like I could her?

"Fancy meeting you here," I said, as I came to rest at her side, leaning one arm on the bar top.

"Jack and Coke, please," I asked the bartender as they looked at me after dropping off Charlotte's glass of wine.

"So, Hayden. What's a guy like you doing in a place like this?"

"I heard about this great cause, supporting the future of independent bookstores, and I wanted to donate."

Charlotte took a sip of her wine as the bartender returned with my drink. I pulled a twenty out of my wallet, putting it in the tip jar. Charlotte made no move to walk away, so I followed her lead, turning my body toward hers.

Charlotte's blue eyes locked on mine, and instantly, I felt like she could see all of me.

"So it has nothing at all to do with my fevered meltdown about losing a major donor?" She sipped a glass of her wine while I decided to lay myself bare.

"I knew I could help. I would have paid the $20,000 to you directly to keep you at home, in bed, resting. I hated seeing you like that and just wanted to do what I could to make it go away."

Charlotte's jaw dropped slightly as her eyes searched my face, seeming to look for any sign I was full of it.

"Well," Charlotte said, a look on her face I couldn't quite decipher. "Thank you. I wouldn't have gotten the rest I did last week if this problem wasn't solved, and more than that, you helped my gala to be a huge success."

The sincerity in her words warmed me from the inside out, not unlike the sip of my drink I took to keep myself from smiling too widely.

"I've got to go snag my boss. It's almost time for her to address everyone. But again, thank you, Hayden."

She turned to walk away, and I felt an immediate sense of loss. I know it was an outlandish gesture to throw that kind of money at the girl you couldn't get out of your head—or at least a cause that was incredibly important to her. I'm not sure what I had expected her reaction to be when she found out I was behind the last-minute donation, but this level-headed, sincere thank you made her glow even brighter in my eyes. I threw out the next thing that came into my head, wanting to spark a reaction to me, not to Duncan's money.

"Save a dance for me?"

She turned back toward me, staying a few feet away.

"Is this Hayden, major donor and CIO of Brandt Investing International, asking? Or Hayden, my roommate, asking?"

"Neither. Well, probably more your roommate. But truly, just Hayden Brandt, asking the most beautiful woman in the room to dance."

Charlotte's cheeks turned a beautiful shade of pink and I found myself wondering where else that pink bloomed on her body.

"Well, you know where to find me."

With that, she turned away and continued her path toward her table. I watched her go, her curves wrapped in a deep ruby that contrasted the way the lights overhead shone on her hair, creating a beacon I couldn't look away from.

Much of the evening wore on before I got to collect on my dance. Being the most senior member of Brandt Investing International at an event like this meant I needed to do some schmoozing, as unnatural as it felt to do so. And it seemed like Charlotte was flitting around talking to everyone and taking care of everything. Everyone wanted to have a moment with the woman responsible for putting together such a fabulous event, and while I would have liked to monopolize her for myself, I was happy to see her receive the accolades she deserved.

Suddenly, the band was announcing the last song for the evening, ending it with something slow. From the other side of the dance floor, Charlotte's gaze locked with mine and I crooked my finger at her, requesting her presence immediately. She shook her head at my antics but made her way to where I was standing.

"You owe me one dance. Remember, ma'am?"

"I do remember. It's the only reason I answered to possibly the corniest beckoning move ever."

"Retire the finger wag to win the ladies over. Noted."

We looked at each other for a moment, and I moved to take Charlotte's right hand, wrapping my other hand around her waist. Charlotte's fingers curled over mine and she placed her left hand on my shoulder, bringing our bodies the closest we had ever been intentionally, if you didn't count when she was delirious with fever. Something felt right having her in my arms.

"It seems like everything went well tonight?" I said, my eyes trained on her face.

Charlotte looked up and met my eyes.

"It did. Thank you again. We really would have had to cut corners without your pledge and..." she trailed off.

"I'm just happy I was in a position to help out this way."

We danced in silence for a few moments. I had waited all evening for this moment and now that I had it, I struggled for words. Maybe it was because I was used to Charlotte, my roommate, on the couch or sitting at the island. This Charlotte, the rockstar of the evening, was... more. It took my breath away. Maybe I could find a way to merge the two.

"So, do you have to stay and do any cleanup?" I asked, finally breaking the silence.

"The caterers should handle most of it. The venue will hold anything that's ours until Monday morning when a few of us can come over and grab it."

"Well, Nationals Park is putting off fireworks tonight. One of their fireworks nights got rained out, and they rescheduled it for tonight to thank the fans for their support through the playoffs. Duncan's rooftop would have a fantastic view. Maybe we could watch them together."

Charlotte looked at my face, doing that searching-for-the-truth-of-me thing again.

"I do like fireworks. I'll check in with Paula," she answered as the song ended.

The band thanked everyone for spending their evening with the IBA and there was no reason for Charlotte to still be in my arms, but I couldn't bring myself to let go of her. We stood looking into each other's eyes—

"Charlotte," the woman who addressed the room after dinner appeared at our side, presumably making her Charlotte's boss.

"Paula, hi!" Charlotte responded, her voice pitched higher than normal, immediately dropping my hand and removing the other from my shoulder, leaving a cold mark in its wake. "This is my roommate... well, Hayden's brother owns the condo I'm staying at in Navy Yard and he's staying there too—"

"Hayden Brandt," I interjected, holding my hand out for a handshake.

"Paula Lapman," Charlotte's boss answered, her eyes bouncing between Charlotte and me. "Thank you, and to your company, for the donation at the eleventh hour. You really saved the night."

"Duncan, my brother, is the CEO and our stepmother is a big supporter of our hometown bookstore, so it was an easy decision. I'm just glad we learned of the opportunity when we did."

Paula looked at me knowingly, not unlike the look Margaret would likely give me if she were here.

"Well, in any case, once again Charlotte, tonight was fantastic. You should head out now. You've already put in twelve hours today, I imagine?"

"Fourteen, actually."

Paula shook her head, admonishing Charlotte gently.

"I'd tell you not to come in until noon on Monday if I had any hopes of that sticking, but at the very least, I insist you leave right now. I imagine Mr. Brandt can see you home safely?"

"Oh, I figured I'd grab a car ho—"

"My car service is on call. He'll be right around the corner.

I'll be sure she gets home in one piece. Do you have a coat to grab?"

Charlotte narrowed her eyes but seemed reluctant to argue with me in front of her boss.

"I do. I'll go grab it and meet you by the elevator?"

"Sounds good. I'll see you then."

Charlotte made her way toward the kitchen, Paula and I both watching after her as she walked away.

Paula looked at me knowingly. "She's a good egg, Mr. Brandt. Be sure you treat her as such."

"Yes ma'am," I responded, reminded more and more of Margaret with each passing moment.

I looked around the room and saw Preston chatting with some of his colleagues. I walked up to him and clapped my hand on his shoulder.

"I imagine you all are heading to some Capitol Hill-friendly bar to continue debating the issues until the wee hours of the morning?"

"Pretty much. I assume you're ditching me to take your *room-mate* home?" Preston responded, his eyes warm and supportive despite his teasing tone.

"Pretty much. Lunch sometime this week?"

"Sounds like a plan. Since you bought dinner tonight, it'll be on me."

Preston and I shook hands as I laughed, both of us knowing it would take twenty lunches to make up for what dinner cost tonight.

I turned away, heading toward the elevator to meet Char-lotte. It was time to watch some fireworks and maybe see if she felt any potential fireworks between us as well.

CHAPTER
Sixteen

CHARLOTTE

The ride home from the gala was silent, both Hayden and I looking out our windows, watching as monuments and government buildings zoomed by on the short ride back to the condo. As we got out of the car at the front door, Hayden said, "The fireworks are set to start in just a couple of minutes, but did you want to change first?"

I weighed my options. The air had turned crisp, but at the same time, I really did love fireworks and didn't want to miss anything.

"I think I'll be okay. Let's go straight to the roof."

Hayden and I moved to the elevator. Once on board, he took a key out of his pocket, slotted it into the control panel and hit the "R" for Roof.

"Why don't I have one of those?" I asked as we ascended the levels of the building. "I didn't even know we could access the roof." The doors opened to an enclosed space with a stainless-steel door ahead of us that presumably led to the roof.

"Only shiny, important owners get a key to the roof and these keys can't be copied. Duncan left it in his office for me to grab."

We pushed the door and walked onto an open rooftop, the

unique skyline of Washington DC on the right behind lanes of highway. Nationals Park stood directly in front of our vantage point, only a few blocks away. Hayden hadn't oversold the view.

"I guess no one else wanted to catch the fireworks tonight?" I asked. Sweeping my head around, I took in that we were alone on the roof.

"Maybe it's super shiny owners. I honestly don't know how many people have access to the roof outside of the staff. I guess if anyone asks what we're doing up here, we can blame it on Duncan. Let him take the fallout."

I felt myself giggling as I approached the edge of the roof, buffeted in by a wall that came mid-chest. Hayden came to stand next to me, keeping a respectable distance, much further than he was when we danced a little while ago. I remembered how the warmth of his palm felt on my waist, knowing he wanted it there, out of necessity as he was walking me to my bedroom, so I didn't pass out. I hadn't known how to broadcast my emotions when I realized Hayden was behind the donation. A multimillion-dollar investing firm had charitable funds to spare, but how sincere Hayden had been when explaining why he donated stirred something in me. The dance only kept my insides twisting. A full-body shiver moved through me now.

"Cold?" Hayden asked, shrugging out of his tux jacket before I could answer. He wrapped it around my shoulders, and I grabbed the lapels, pulling it tight around my body. It *was* a little chilly up here, and now I was surrounded by the smell of Hayden. And I wasn't going to complain and make it go away.

The fireworks started in the distance and we stood in silence for a few moments, taking in their colors.

"So, away from all your colleagues and the donors, how do you feel about tonight?" Hayden's eyes were on me while I kept watching the fireworks in the distance.

"I'm a bit in denial that it's over, I think. I've been working toward the gala the entire time I've been at the IBA. Now we'll turn to the end-of-the-year fundraising push, but this could be it.

My future at the IBA isn't guaranteed, but I *liked* the work I did ahead of the gala. It's so different from what I left behind in my day-to-day in Holly Ridge, and I think I'm *good* at it. I know I'm good at bookselling and could be good at running a store, but this is something that I've chosen, not something that chose me. And that really makes a difference to me, you know?"

Hayden kept his eyes on me momentarily before turning his head back toward the fireworks.

"I can relate to that feeling a bit. Though I'm the opposite. I'm here, working for Duncan, because I feel like I need to. After our mom died... Duncan stopped being a kid so the rest of us could continue our childhood. He's the one who nudged me toward computers in the first place, and I've never really looked back. I put off taking the CIO position as long as I could, but eventually, the guilt took over. And now, I only touch a computer to answer emails or read reports. Everyone else takes care of security or programming or anything that actually drew me to computers in the first place. Plus, all this concrete, all the buildings and high-rises..." He sighs. "I've lived in a city for the past twelve years and I'm realizing I hate it."

I looked up at his handsome profile, his windswept hair, and took in the fireworks reflecting in his eyes.

"If you could be anywhere, where would you be?"

Hayden turned, taking a step toward me and tucking a piece of my hair behind my ear that the wind had worked free.

"Right now? I want to be right where I am."

Hayden's hand stayed in my hair, running his fingers through the locks until he reached my shoulder, curling his fingers behind my neck, his pointer finger circling gently at my nape. His eyes searched my face, straying to my mouth, broadcasting his intentions. I felt myself swallow, and his eyes followed the motion down between the lapels of his suit jacket. Not wanting him to feel alone in this moment, I took a small step closer to his body, tangling the fingers of his free hand with mine.

The grand finale illuminated the sight of Hayden's face

growing closer to mine before my eyes closed, his lips gently meeting mine—once, twice—before drawing back. The loss of his lips caused my eyes to reopen slowly, reading the question in his. I closed the distance between us this time. My arms circled his neck, and his hand came to rest around my waist as the booms and bursts of the fireworks on the horizon ended and migrated behind my eyes, to this kiss. Hayden's tongue traced the seam of my lips, asking for entry, and I opened gladly, tangling my tongue with his as my grip on his collar tightened.

A groan issued from deep in Hayden's chest sent a rush of wetness to the already damp cloth between my legs, and Hayden rotated us, so I was pressed up against the same wall I had observed earlier. The top of the wall pressed into my shoulder blades. That alone would have been enough to keep me feeling safe from a fall to the street below, but Hayden's arms around me felt as if they would have provided that security on the side of a mountain. And yet, just as the feeling of security registered, a companion emotion appeared: fear. In my thirty-odd years of life, a kiss had never brought so much color into my world, and that terrified me. I left Holly Ridge seeking something more, but never expected this much.

As if Hayden sensed the turmoil in me, his ravenous kisses slowed, but didn't stop immediately. He treated kissing like a high-endurance sport—a cool-down period was necessary.

When our mouths parted, he kept his body close to mine, allowing him to feel the full-body shiver that moved through me.

"Still cold after all that?" he asked, his hands securely grasped my waist, his face displaying his full—and appropriately earned—confidence in his kissing abilities.

I suddenly found myself unable to meet his eyes, while at the same time, I couldn't remove my hands from where they rested on his arms. Hayden resolved that for me by stepping back, his hands trailing from my waist and removing him from my reach. The loss of his body heat caused me to shiver again, this time from the crisp late October air.

"Come on, let's get back inside. I'm sure you're exhausted."

I nodded, still silent, and with my eyes downcast, the weight of the moment, the night, the week, the last few months weighing on me.

We made the journey back to our shared condo in silence. The reflection of the elevator walls betrayed the sneaking glances we both made at each other. Hayden seemed to follow my lead and didn't look directly at me, like I was an easily spooked cat.

He unlocked the door and held it open so I could cross the threshold ahead of him, hanging my bag on the hook inside the door. I broke our silence by groaning in relief as I removed my shoes, the total exhaustion of my body and mind winning out over all other feelings.

Hayden chuckled from his position behind me.

"I've never understood how anyone can wear heels like that for an extended period. Don't get me wrong, they look amazing, but dangerous."

"Beauty is pain, Hayden. Never forget that. Plus, I've been on my feet several hours a day, five or more days a week, since I was sixteen. I haven't felt my feet in years."

We moved into the living area together.

"Do you want something to drink? Wine? Or maybe some tea?" Hayden looked a little lost, while also appearing relieved that we were talking again.

"Honestly? I just want to sleep for a million years."

Hayden nodded. "That makes sense. I probably should turn in too, or at least get out of this monkey suit."

My mind went to Hayden, stripping out of that tux while I watched. Or better yet, as I helped and licked his skin as it was revealed.

"Charlotte?"

Hayden was halfway down the hallway, looking at me with concern as I had stayed grounded in place. I shook the X-rated images out of my head and smiled, walking toward him and continuing until I reached the door of my room.

"Goodnight, Hayden," I said as I gripped the doorknob to enter, feeling a hand on my arm.

Hayden turned me in his arms and wrapped his arms around me, enveloping me in a tight hug.

"You were amazing tonight. You should be really proud of yourself and everything you've accomplished." His words were a balm I didn't know I needed. In our house growing up, hard work and efforts weren't praised, they were expected. For someone to notice my work and acknowledge it out loud, it meant everything.

I took in a shuddering breath as I felt his lips graze my forehead, and he let me break out of his grip. Moving to close my bedroom door behind me, putting a physical barrier between myself and the temptation to undo all of my plans, Hayden's "Goodnight, Charlotte" snuck in before I closed the door with a snap. I leaned against the wooden barrier, listening to the silence in the hallway behind me until I heard Hayden's door close as well. Only then did I give up my vigil post and go about getting to bed, wondering perhaps if there was a way I could have more than I ever thought I deserved.

CHAPTER
Seventeen

HAYDEN

I woke up when the sky was just light enough to peek through the cracks in my curtains, alerting me that another morning had risen. *The morning isn't alone in that,* I thought wryly, looking down my body to where the sheet was tented. It had been hard and yet so easy to let Charlotte go to her room last night. Something had shut down in her after our amazing kiss. While I would have loved to feel more of her against me, either vertically or horizontally, something held her back. So, I went to my room, alone, and laid in bed. Much like now, I hadn't allowed myself to touch my rigid cock, even though the scent of Charlotte lingered on my skin. I fell back on the age-old, code-something-in-your-head trick, a computer nerd's version of counting sheep, and finally drifted off.

In the grey morning light, I thought back to how at peace I felt with Charlotte on the roof, revealing to her how out of my element I felt at my job and in the city. With cheeks rosy from the wind, the bright lights of the fireworks, and Charlotte's, well Charlotte-ness, how could I not kiss her? And the way she kissed me back...

I groaned, my hand palming my cock through the sheet out of reflex.

No, I thought, my eyes snapping open, ripping the sheet off my naked body and making my way to the shower, where I turned the water on cold and stepped right in. Pressing my palms up against the tile, I rested my weight there, hanging my head, letting the cold water work away my morning wood. Charlotte's face may have flashed in my mind innocuously before during some solo-sessions, but now that I knew what it was like to have her hands on other parts of me, feel her lips against mine, I wanted to build something with her. Not use thoughts of her as a method of quick release when I wasn't sure I'd get the chance to touch her like that again.

I switched the water to warm and finished washing my body and hair in no time flat, needing to get out of a situation where anything dangled dangerously. I got dressed and headed out to the kitchen to make coffee, wondering what to do with my Saturday. Part of me wanted to wait around the apartment to see what Charlotte's plans for the day were. Another part of me said that was pathetic and maybe a little creepy, especially given she mentioned her hope to sleep in.

I looked at my running shoes by the door and my work bag hanging from an island chair while I waited for my coffee to finish brewing. None of that called to me the way sitting on the couch and pretending to watch college football pre-shows until Charlotte came out of her room did. *Slightly creepy Saturday morning, it is.*

Taking my coffee to the couch, I turned the TV on but made sure the volume was low enough it couldn't possibly disturb my roommate. *Maybe I should go get donuts? Or bagels? Or something? But then what if she leaves and I miss her?*

I put my hands to my face, groaning into them. Who was this person she turned me into?

"Everything okay there, champ?"—I jumped—"Did you

suddenly gain supersonic hearing or something? Why's the TV so low?"

"No supersonic hearing, though glad your ninja powers are intact. I just didn't want to wake you."

Charlotte laughed. "Sorry I scared you. You okay on coffee or need more?"

She made her way to the coffee machine, which gave me a chance to look at her fully. I wasn't sure if things would be awkward this morning or not. So far, so good. She didn't look tense from behind.

"I'm okay. I just got this cup. I didn't expect you up so early."

"I didn't think I would be either, but I passed out basically as soon as my head hit the pillow, and when I woke up, I felt well-rested. I guess six solid hours of sleep is an improvement on three or four hours of stress sleep."

Charlotte sipped her coffee from where she leaned against the front of the kitchen island, facing me in the living room. Her hair was sleep-tousled, her face free of makeup, and she looked relaxed and at ease for the first time in weeks. But she claimed she fell asleep right away? Was it not awkward right now because she was going to pretend our kiss never happened? Because that just wouldn't do.

"So, what are you up to today?" I asked as I stretched my arms over my head in a way that I knew would reveal the sliver of stomach above the band of my joggers. I watched Charlotte's eyes take in that span of skin as she licked her lips. That was better.

"Uh... today. Yes." Charlotte blinked, her eyes back on mine. "I realized I've been here for two months and haven't had a chance to explore anything outside the district. So, I thought I'd hop over to Virginia and check out Old Town Alexandria. It looks so cute in photos. There's supposed to be a great independent bookstore there, and lots of neat restaurants and coffee shops."

"Oh, that sounds like fun. I've been wanting to check out Old Town too. Head out in thirty minutes?"

I finished the final swig of coffee in my mug and went to set it in the sink.

"Oh, uh, you want to come? I figured you'd have to work? You've been working weekends recently..."

I walked up to Charlotte and set my fingers under her chin, bringing her eyes up to meet mine.

"Not last weekend, remember? And before that, I didn't want to be here and not be... well, be with you. So, is it okay if I spend the day with you?"

Charlotte nodded, moving my fingers up and down with her chin, her eyes wide.

I felt a broad smile cross my face.

"Great. See you in thirty."

"Can we make it an hour? I'd really like to shower before we head out and not feel rushed."

"Of course. Take all the time you need," I said with meaning.

I bent to pop a quick kiss on Charlotte's forehead before heading back to my room, leaving her stunned in the kitchen. I wasn't going to let her pretend something wasn't happening here. I'd respect the uncertainty I felt within her last night and go slow, but if she didn't want this, Charlotte would have to use her big girl words to say so.

A little over an hour later, Charlotte and I were exiting onto the street in front of our building. It was crisp and sunny, a perfect day for exploring a new place with your current favorite person. Charlotte was dressed in a bright pink sweater and deep teal puffy vest that made her blue eyes shine. Her jeans made her ass look fantastic, and they were tucked into boots that came up to her knees. A few too many layers, maybe, but she looked so fucking cute.

"So, how are we getting to Old Town?" I asked, sliding my sunglasses on to protect from the bright autumn rays.

"The Metro?" Charlotte asked, pointing in the direction we would need to head to enter the closest station.

"What if we took the Potomac Water Taxi over from the Wharf? I bet the trees look great, and it shouldn't be too windy on the water today."

"Oh, sure. I didn't realize that was an option. I do miss the New England foliage this fall. It's the first time I won't get to see Holly Ridge change colors."

"Well then, we have to take the water taxi. I'll order a car to get us over to the dock."

I took out my phone to do just that and saw I had some messages from Duncan, but I ignored them. Just because he was working on a Saturday didn't mean I had to.

"Car will be here in two minutes," I announced, looking up from my phone to see Charlotte looking at me quizzically.

"What are you doing, Hayden?"

"Getting us to the Wharf? Water taxi, pretty leaves, scenic views?"

"No, I mean, why are you coming to Old Town with me? And suggesting longer, if not prettier, ways to get there?"

"I just want to spend the day with you, Charlotte, and thought you might like the boat ride. It's still your day, whatever you want to do."

"So, if I want to spend an hour in the bookstore, that's fine?"

"I'll even carry your stack of books for you."

"And if I want to stop in every boutique?"

"We'll be able to recommend our favorites to anyone who asks."

"What about dinner? What if I only want ice cream?"

"I hope one of those boutiques has some lactose pills for sale, but it's your call."

Charlotte continued to look at me, her lips turning up

slightly, her eyes sparkling with amusement at my willingness to join in her whatever she had planned for the day.

"It's your day, Char. Whatever you want. Here comes the car. Are we doing this?"

A full smile broke out across Charlotte's face.

"Okay, fine. For today, we're doing this."

I opened the car door for Charlotte to get in, walking around to the other side to slide in myself, feeling a matching smile on my face. Today was a start.

Charlotte and I grabbed sandwiches from Chopsmith to enjoy on the boat ride as an early lunch. After boarding, we grabbed seats on the top deck facing the open water to the south, enjoying the warm October sun on our faces.

"So, why don't I know you from Holly Ridge High?" Charlotte asked, before taking a large bite of her lobster roll, chewing while she waited for my answer.

"My dad and Margaret got married the summer after I graduated from high school. I guess a bunch of my stuff moved to Holly Ridge, but only Hunter and Spencer made the actual move with them that summer. I went straight to Boston for college and only visited during the winter break."

Charlotte nodded. "That makes sense. And it's madness that time of year because of the Christmas festival, so even if we did run into each other, I would have thought you were just another tourist."

"I bet all the tourist boys flock to Ridge Reads to see the pretty woman behind the counter, especially when she has mayonnaise on her face," I said with a smile as I handed her a napkin from my lap.

Charlotte wiped her face. "Please. Something this messy wasn't allowed anywhere near the cash wrap. It might get on the books! My mom is a real stickler like that. Protein bars were my main form of sustenance when I couldn't get away long enough for a real meal."

"What was it like, growing up in a bookstore?"

Charlotte took a drink from her water bottle, taking in the scenery before answering.

"Honestly, for a lot of my life, I loved it. I never stood a chance to be anything other than a bookworm, given our family's livelihood. But it felt magical to grow up in a building filled with books, where other people would visit us to talk about them and take my favorites home.

"I think I was ten when I made my first book recommendation. A little boy was standing next to his mom, whining that he didn't want to try *The Baby-Sitters Club* because those books were for girls. He just wanted the next *Goosebumps* book. I marched right up to him and let him know that if he really wanted something scary, he should think about the fact that the babysitters had created a small business and wouldn't need boys to take them out for milkshakes. Then I whirled right around and went back to alphabetizing biographies or something. I remember my dad laughing at me from the counter, but when he told my mom about it at dinner that night, she asked what they ended up buying. She was mad when Dad admitted nothing—the boy needed more time to think about what he wanted to read next."

Charlotte sighed and looked down at her empty sandwich wrappings, crumpling them into a small ball with her hands, fidgeting as she spoke.

"I haven't thought about that in a really long time. I love my mom. I mean, she's my mom, but her love of books warped into something tied up in money and bottom lines, and not being about the love of books anymore. She's an only child too and grew up in the store, just like I have. When I felt my love of books starting to morph in the same way, I knew I needed to do something different."

We sat in silence for a few moments. It didn't feel like she was seeking affirmation or reassurance, but was weighing her family situation out loud. I touched Charlotte's hand to still her movements under the guise of taking the wrappings so I could toss them along with mine in the trash can a few feet from where we sat. I also hoped it might let her know someone was on her side.

"So, only child, huh? I guess that explains why you're so spoiled," I teased gently as I settled back on the bench beside her, hoping to lift the mood.

"I resent that stereotype, Hayden Brandt. What about you? You're the rebellious middle-child, huh?"

I laughed. "I may be the literal middle Brandt brother, being the older twin, but Hunter got all the rebellious genes, believe me. Though, if you talked to anyone from our hometown, they'd probably say we shared that trait, because I rarely let Hunter get into trouble by himself when we were kids. We were eight when our mom died, and that's the way Hunter dealt with his emotions. He just didn't. He's still a little like that, though he stopped dragging me into his shenanigans once we hit high school."

"Now you drag him into schemes to sell fake llamas on the internet. What a way to repay him."

I felt my cheeks warm at the reference to the gone-so-wrong prank. I looked over at Charlotte to see a teasing glint in her eyes and felt myself relax.

"Yeah, I guess maybe I do have a bit of that middle child syndrome left in me, after all."

A voice came over the loudspeaker, letting us know we'd be arriving at the dock in Old Town in five minutes.

Charlotte looked surprised. "Wow, that trip seemed to take no time at all."

"I lose track of time all the time when I'm with you, Charlotte."

A blush darkened her cheeks, already rosy from the elements. I tucked a windswept piece of hair behind her ear again. I would take any opportunity I could to touch her casually, not wanting to cross too far. The sudden jarring motion of the boat meeting the side of the dock broke us out of the moment and I put my hand back on my thigh.

"So"—she stood, getting ready to leave the boat—"please tell this only child more stories about what it was like to grow up with four brothers."

I stood up to join her.

"I'll start with the blackmail stories about Preston. I'm sure he'll return the favor whenever you two meet. It's only a matter of time after the gala."

"When?" Charlotte looked at me, seeming shocked by my certainty. I smiled. It had been a long time since my brothers had met a woman who meant something to me. Preston, being geographically closest, would absolutely volunteer as tribute, especially since he was the nosiest one of the bunch.

"Yes, Charlotte. When. Now, let's go get you some books."

CHAPTER
Eighteen

CHARLOTTE

Hayden and I walked up King Street from the waterfront, heading toward the bookstore I had heard about. Hayden kept me laughing with stories about Preston and his other brothers that were somewhat childish and embarrassing, but endearing. What I really took away from them was how much love the brothers shared for each other, even if they were no longer all under one roof. I knew my parents loved me, but we didn't have many family memories that didn't involve the bookstore as well. Hayden, his brothers, and their dad had lost so much, but had never forgotten what remained.

Was it the certainty there would be a brother to pick up the phone when he called that gave Hayden the confidence this thing between us would work out—the very thing I was trying to ignore? I figured pretending the kiss from last night didn't happen was the least awkward way to not address it, but Hayden seemed determined to respect my boundaries while also being sure I knew he wasn't giving up.

"Charlotte?"

I looked around, standing at the edge of the sidewalk ready to cross another street, but Hayden was no longer beside me.

"The bookstore is down this way, I think?"

I looked up at the street sign and saw he was right.

"Thanks, I was just…" I trailed off, turning to join him, continuing down the sidewalk.

"I knew the story about making mud pies naked in the back-yard was one too many."

I laughed. "No, no it's not that, it's just…" Would I ever finish a sentence today?

Hayden looked down at me. "I know."

And he did seem to know, without me even saying anything, and was content to wait for me to figure my jumbled head out.

Hayden put his hand on my lower back, guiding me through the door to heaven—a.k.a. a bookstore—where all problems, like handsome men who were too sweet and understanding for me to handle, didn't exist.

I breathed in. "Do you smell that?"

Hayden inhaled. "Smell what?"

"It's books! The best smell in the world."

Hayden sniffed again. "I don't smell it?"

I looked at him aghast, grabbing a basket from where they were stashed inside the door. "We're just going to have to stay here until you do."

Hayden laughed, taking in the different sections, one room blending into another in the cozy and intimate space.

"I'm going to find their business section," Hayden said, jerking his head in the direction of one of the other rooms.

"I'm going to start out here, take the whole space in," I responded, not looking at him anymore as I took in the tables in the front room lined with new releases. I felt slightly out of touch, not having put out new releases at Ridge Reads for over three months. There was some standout I had missed in that gap. I'd need to peruse slowly.

I lost myself in the feeling of enjoying a bookstore that I had no personal stake in, other than being a book lover. Even as I leaned into the immersion of browsing, my brain couldn't help take in the little details that seemed to stand out to make this store so successful. A busy events calendar, personal recommendations for books hanging from the shelves, friendly staff. My professional mind whirred with ideas about workshops for struggling independent bookstores across the country.

Eventually, even those thoughts faded into the background as I wandered the sections slowly, stopping to read recommendations of titles marked by staff as their favorites. I crossed into another room, looking around briefly for Hayden. When I didn't see him, I lost myself in browsing a highly anticipated memoir I hadn't had a chance to flip through yet. I added it to my basket. It was now so heavy, I set it down and pushed the basket with my foot to a new spot on the floor as I moved along.

I jumped slightly when I felt a hand on my shoulder. Turning, I saw Hayden standing there. "I believe I promised to hold your book stack for you. Sorry to make you lug it around. Duncan called after sending me a text ordering me to answer his call and I just finished putting out that fire." Hayden lifted the basket with one hand, his other running through his hair.

Good to know those weren't just show muscles, I mused.

"Must have been a small fire," I said, checking my watch. "Orrrr not. Shit! It's already been an hour? Okay, I'm done." I moved to take the basket back from Hayden so I could head to the register and check out.

"No, you're not. You haven't even made it into the last room yet. I just wanted to grab your basket. I'm going to go sit at that table over there and look at that new Barefoot Contessa cookbook. I know Margaret wants it for Christmas, but she and my dad are trying to eat gluten-free, so I want to be sure the recipes are easily adaptable." Hayden gestured toward said table with his head and turned to move in that direction. I grabbed his arm to stop him and raised up on my toes to plant a kiss on his cheek.

"Thank you," I said.

Hayden's eyes warmed at my sudden burst of affection.

"Anytime, my lady." His eyes widened. "Not that you're my lady... I mean, if you wanted..."

"Smooth," I laughed. "Go look at your cookbook. I promise I won't be too much longer."

"Take all the time you need." This time, when he turned toward the corner he had identified, I let him go.

This one's got stamina, I thought, feeling myself heat at the thought of what all types of stamina he might have. I hurried toward the kids' books, because few things were less horny than books aimed at tiny humans who were just learning to read.

After another thirty minutes or so, I really was ready to go, and I went to grab Hayden so we could get checked out and continue on with our day. I noticed he had moved on from the cookbook, which sat on top of my basket of books, and was now thirty pages deep in *Bird by Bird* by Anne Lamott.

"Going to write the great American novel, Brandt?"

Hayden jumped, making us even for jump scares this afternoon. He marked his page with a piece of paper from his pocket and added the book to the pile.

"I don't think so. I remember Ted Lasso referencing the book, and I thought I'd check it out. I don't think writing's my path, but I wonder if I'm looking at my unhappiness with being CIO as too large a problem and I need to break it down bird by bird first. I'll see Duncan in December and think maybe I should talk to him then."

I smiled at Hayden, noticing how handsome he looked when he was feeling determined about something.

"Looks like we both got something out of this bookstore trip then," I said, hoisting up the pile of gifts and other books I had added to my arms since Hayden relieved me of my basket.

Hayden's eyes widened. "We're going to need another boat to get all those back across the river."

I shrugged. "I know it's a lot, but we get a monthly reimbursement from work for purchases at an indie bookstore when we submit receipts and I haven't submitted anything yet. Plus, a lot of these are gifts. It's hard to surprise bookstore owners with books from their own inventory, ya know? Maybe we can leave them behind the counter until we're ready to head back, so we don't have to lug them around all afternoon. We'll see what time they close."

"I'll help carry them, if not. It's no trouble. I'm glad you found so much to buy. It's a great store. We should support them."

I winced. "Sorry, reflex. I've dated oth—I mean, had friends who didn't understand why I would buy so much from another bookstore when I had access to any book I wanted at our store."

With that, I turned around and headed toward the front before I could stick my foot in my mouth any further. I heard his chair scrape on the floor as he stood to follow me and we weaved our way around the other customers enjoying a casual Saturday among the books.

I joined the line at the register, inhaling the scent of Hayden's cologne as he came to stand close behind me.

"Hi there," the young woman behind the register greeted us. "Looks like y'all were successful today."

"You have a great selection of stuff here," I said, setting the stack in my arms on the counter and starting to unload the rest from the basket Hayden held.

"It's one of my favorite parts of working at an indie, that we have control over curation of titles," the young woman responded. The beep of the scanner created a familiar rhythm, giving me a pang of homesickness.

"It's one reason I love stopping in every indie bookstore I come across," I answered, pulling my card out to pay for my purchases. "We can share a bag, or well, bags, by the way. We're headed to the same place."

I moved aside so Hayden could pay for his books, putting my wallet back in my purse.

"Are you parked close?" the bookseller asked as she put a

bookmark into Hayden's books and slid them into the bag with some of mine.

Hayden and I exchanged a glance, both of us smiling.

"We're just on this side of the river for the afternoon. We took the water taxi over. Can you hold these purchases for a little while?"

"We can," she answered. "But we also have a delivery service, depending on where exactly you live. We can have these delivered to your home in the next couple of days."

"Let's do that," Hayden cut in. "You can put that on my card with my books. It'll be worth it, even though it means I'll still have to do arm day tomorrow morning."

The bookseller laughed, eyeing Hayden's arms. The hunter-green sweater he wore clung to his muscles.

Had to show those things off, didn't you, Hayden?

"Charlotte, did you want to grab a book to start this weekend, just in case it's a few days before the rest get dropped off?" Hayden asked, looking at me expectantly.

He calmed my hackles with a simple question. The bookseller now directed her smile at me, her face seeming to say, *you have a man who gets it*.

"I would, thank you," I answered softly. I dragged the bag with my fiction purchases toward me, deciding which one I wanted to bring with me while Hayden and the bookseller worked out the delivery details.

Tucking the witchy rom-com with plenty of spice that was blowing up online right now into my purse, I looked up to see Hayden taking his receipt back from the bookseller.

"We'll send you an email with when to expect the books. The delivery schedule will be updated tomorrow morning following the weekend. Thanks so much for stopping in." The bookseller waved goodbye, as Hayden interlaced his fingers with mine, guiding us out of the store.

"That's a good idea, coordinating with a courier service to deliver books within a certain radius," Hayden mused, looking at the business card the young woman had attached to his receipt. "We've received deliveries from this service at the office before. Anyway"—he tucked the receipt into his pocket—"where to?"

We walked back toward the main drag of town, my hand tucked in his like we strolled hand-in-hand through quaint city streets every weekend. And while that wasn't true, it strangely felt like it could be.

CHAPTER
Nineteen

HAYDEN

It was hard to think of an afternoon more perfect than this one. Charlotte and I had been unintentional roommates for two months now. I knew more than what you could glean from a few conversations with her, like the fact that she was a hell of a prankster or that she sang in the shower. But this afternoon together showed me so much more. She saw people around her, pointing out couples and asking me what I thought their backstory was. And more than once, I saw her take her phone out as we exited a store. After the third time she did it, I had to know and asked what she was doing.

"I have a running file of small business ideas that I think could help Ridge Reads or really any independent bookstore. One of the roadmap ideas for the Independent Bookstore Fund is to offer consulting services along with the grants. When Paula and I meet at the end of my internship to discuss if there's a position available for me to stay with the IBA, I want to be prepared for all opportunities, including heading up that effort. I figure taking notes when something strikes me out in the real world can't hurt."

I stood next to her outside the pet boutique we had just

exited, looking between the window display of fall accessories for small dogs and the woman in front of me sliding her phone back into her pocket.

"What?" she asked, smiling shyly.

"I'm just amazed that you can see something in a store like this one, that's so different from a bookstore and transform it into something useful."

Charlotte shrugged. "They're all small businesses supporting a niche in the community. The product may be different, but the target experience to serve the people who patronize and lift it up is the same."

"You're amazing," I said, smiling down at her, finding myself reaching for her hand again to tangle my fingers with hers, brushing my thumb across the top of her hand. Charlotte gave my hand a squeeze, trying and failing to suppress a smile at my praise. That may be the fourth time in twenty-four hours I said something similar, but with a woman like this, I had to let her know.

"You're just delusional from hunger, I think," Charlotte said, tugging on our linked hands, starting us down the sidewalk back toward the water again. "Let's find somewhere for dinner?"

"Amazing and full of excellent ideas at that," I said, giving her hand a squeeze back. "You in the mood for anything in particular?"

"I overheard the girls working at that place talking about a killer margarita, so I, of course, asked them where I could find said marg. They suggested a place just down here, if that sounds okay?"

"You'll never hear me complain about Mexican food. Let's throw in some guacamole for the table, though."

Charlotte smiled up at me. "You're on."

We walked in comfortable silence the couple of blocks to the restaurant. The hostess directed us to a table outside, on the edge of the road closed to car traffic, with a heater blowing warm air. The sun had set while we meandered through shops and the evening air turned colder, but with the benefit of modern outdoor dining amenities, it would be lovely to eat on the street and continue to people watch.

Margaritas and guac ordered, Charlotte and I ignored the menu, trading off stories for the couples we saw dining at the restaurants around us. All that time spent in imaginary worlds and backstories was good for her creativity. Her contributions were much stronger than mine.

The waiter visited our table for the third time before we decided we better focus on food, the margaritas made us feel loosened and extra giddy. For me, I knew part of that was my proximity to Charlotte, in addition to the tequila.

Our food and another round of drinks arrived in no time, and we were silent for a few moments, the sound of silverware clinking and conversations from our fellow diners creating ambient noise while we dug into our meals.

"So," Charlotte started, taking a sip from her water glass to wash down the spice from her enchiladas. "I know you're just starting to look at the birds, but you're a smart guy. If you're not CIO or working for Duncan, what do you want to do? Something still with computers?"

"You know how I told you last night that Duncan was the one to push me toward computers in the first place? Part of the reason for that, beyond it keeping me in the house and accounted for, was that he knew I would be able to make a living. After Mom died, Dad worked a lot. Part of it, I think, was to keep from feeling lonely and sad, but he also needed to make sure we had enough. I mean, we didn't have Air Force Ones or anything, but we also never went hungry or without new sneakers at the start of the school year. But honestly, keeping us in food was hard enough. Do you know how much five boys eat?"

Charlotte laughed gently, her hand reaching out to cover mine on top of the table.

"Duncan made sure we stayed in line, well as much as a teenager could. Dad wouldn't let him get an official job to help out, but if there was a lawn he didn't mow or driveway he didn't shovel on our street, I'd be shocked. So, when Hunter started getting into trouble in high school, and I wasn't sure how to help my best friend, Duncan suggested I take a free coding class on the family's computer, something to distract me and lose myself in. Turns out, I was really good at it, and he encouraged it, because like I said, I could make a living doing those things.

"But then, after Dad married Margaret, who holds the patents for several coffee-machine-related inventions, money wasn't a worry anymore. I had worked hard so I could get a scholarship to cover school, but suddenly, there was money to allow me to go to a more prestigious university and pay the difference that a partial scholarship wouldn't cover. It's hard to shake the feeling that you need to work as hard as you can to stay on the path and pay the man. Duncan feeds on that sort of energy, which is why his company is so damn successful. But me? I think I need something more than a fancy title and salary that goes along with it."

I took a drink of my margarita, suddenly aware that I wasn't sure I had ever said so many words in a row to Charlotte at one time.

She rested her chin on her hand, the one that wasn't still resting on mine on the table. I flipped my hand over to grasp hers more fully.

"So, then, what *does* mean something to you?"

"Well, last night Paula mentioned something in her keynote about technological advances and how it's important for book-stores to keep up, even though it's a difficult learning curve for the owners sometimes. While I was listening to you sing in the shower this morning—"

"Hey!" Charlotte exclaimed, shoving me gently with the hand I had been holding before settling back in her chair, picking up her margarita with both hands. While I missed the warmth of her touch, I felt her full attention on what I was saying.

"I realized that was probably the case in a lot of industries.

Then you mentioned the consulting the Bookstore Future Fund has on its road map. Somewhere between last night's keynote, *Bird by Bird,* and walking around interacting with all of these businesses, I think there might be a real need for technology consulting for small businesses to keep them competitive and up to date. It may be too hard to be super broad, so I may need to find a niche, but it's just an idea that's brewing right now."

Charlotte looked at me, her eyes filling with what I read as resignation.

"Have you ever shopped at my parent's store?"

I looked around at the abrupt subject change, trying to see what sparked it.

Charlotte laughed. "Sorry, tequila brain, and being too inside my head. It's related, I promise."

I shook my head. "I haven't, but I know Margaret loves it."

Charlotte smiled. "A lot of people in Holly Ridge do, but that's as far as their reach goes. Margaret calls in her book orders, like a lot of our other regulars, because we don't have a website where you can order online. My parents have had to embrace some technology, to keep up with ordering new releases and replacing stock, but there are some things they're absolutely resistant to. I can't make them see reason, but I think they could benefit from something exactly like what you're talking about. A technology embracement audit." She shook her head. "Technology embracement audit, that's terrible, but what I'm trying to say is I think you're on to something here. It's a need, and I can tell from how you talk about it, it could make you happy."

I realized I was happy and excited thinking about this nugget of an idea, much happier than I had been thinking about work in a long time.

"I think you might be right."

At this point, the waiter asked if we were ready for our check, and after confirming glances at each other, I told him we were. I handed him my card, taking away the opportunity for Charlotte to pay.

"Very smooth, Mr. Brandt. I bet you pull that move with all the girls."

"There aren't any other girls, Charlotte. There haven't been since you ran into me, brandishing a purse as a weapon while I was wearing a towel."

Charlotte seemed speechless, and the waiter returned with my card and copy to sign, breaking the moment.

"Want to take the water taxi back? Or opt for the more direct option of taking a car the whole way home?" I held my hand out to help Charlotte out of her seat.

"Let's go for the water taxi," Charlotte said, seeming to want to extend our day as much as I did.

Charlotte tucked her arm through mine, bringing her body closer. Maybe she was seeking heat, but I liked to think she also wanted to be near me.

We got to the dock to learn the next boat was leaving in a few moments, having timed things just right. We bought our tickets and climbed back to the top deck. Charlotte walked to the edge, taking in the view of National Harbor to the southeast and the Washington Monument and National Cathedral to the north. I stopped a bit away from her, taking in her profile as her head turned this way and that, soaking in how much I'd enjoyed this day and how much I hoped she had too.

She turned her head over her shoulder and caught me watching her, encouraging me toward her with a bob of her head. "Come on over, Hayden. Guess we won't see any leaves this time, but the lights sure are pretty."

I stepped forward to stand beside her and I felt the boat shudder as the engine started and we pushed away from the dock. Charlotte shivered next to me, her arms coming up to grip her sleeves where they were exposed under her vest.

I moved to stand directly behind her, placing my hands outside of hers on the railing, resting the side of my head on the top of hers. Charlotte seemed to lean part of her weight back against me, and I heard her sigh.

"So, did you have a good day?"

"I had the best day."

"Good, I'm glad." I smiled against the top of her head, wondering if she would be able to tell and know she was responsible.

"Hayden?"

"Yeah?"

She turned around in my arms, so my grasp on the railing bracketed her torso against mine. I saw her look behind me on cither side, and pleased with what she found, she brought her hands up to rest on my chest.

"I know I said we could have today. And after today, I would very much like to have a tomorrow, but I came here to accomplish a goal, to prove to my parents, and to myself, that I could do more than just run a bookstore in our small town. I wasn't expecting a roommate, and I wasn't expecting that roommate to be you and for you to offer... this."

She buried her face in her hands, leaving my chest feeling cold and incomplete without them.

"Gosh, I'm saying this all wrong. Stupid tequila and intoxicating Hayden scent."

I removed my hands from the railing to gently tug hers from her face, tangling our fingers together at our sides.

"You can't afford for a distraction."

"That makes what you have to offer sound so cheap, and it's not. Hayden, you're amazing, but—"

"But you don't know where you're going, and now you know I don't exactly know where I'm going."

Charlotte nodded. "Yes, exactly. I've never taken a chance on myself, betting on me, before. And if I didn't see that through, I'd never forgive myself."

I squeezed Charlotte's hands in mine.

"I understand."

Charlotte searched my face. "So, like I was saying, I said we could have today. And I think I need today to end when we get off this boat, because you know, we live together, and you look like you do, and you smell so fucking amazing—what *is* that, by the way?"

I smiled. "It's Mister Babe. A dumb name, but the smell is unmatched. And I get what you're saying."

I went to step back, but Charlotte held tight to my hands and tugged on them, pulling me so I was flush against her.

"So, we're agreed then, when the boat docks, our perfect day ends."

Before I could verbalize my agreement, Charlotte dropped my hands and wrapped hers around my neck, pulling my mouth down to hers. My brain engaged quickly, considering how much of my blood flow was now headed south, and I wrapped my arms tight around her back, feeling every curve and bend that made up this glorious woman.

Her tongue demanded entrance into my mouth and a groan escaped me, making me pull back and look around.

Charlotte grabbed my head, her lips deliciously red and inviting. "We're the only ones stupid enough to be up here," she said, before bringing my mouth crashing back down on hers.

Our tongues tangled, our mouths moving in a fervor that was different from last night's kiss. That one was full of questions and longing, while this one was powered by desire and a stopwatch.

I pried my mouth from Charlotte's to pepper kisses down her neck, tugging her sweater down to lick at her collarbone before repeating the path back to her lips. The moan this time was hers, one I gladly gobbled up with my mouth, wondering how many more I could earn before we docked.

Charlotte's hands wandered down my back, halting their journey at my ass. Her hands were tucked into my back pockets as she wrapped one of her legs around the back of mine, pulling my hardness into her center. I ground my hips into her core, wanting her to feel exactly what she did to me. Charlotte groaned again, rubbing herself on the hardness trapped in my jeans, trying to find the right angle, the right rhythm. I placed my hands under her ass, not able to stop myself from squeezing before moving on to my original task. Lifting Charlotte up so her ass rested on the second rung from the top of the guardrail, so she had a bit more height. One of my arms moved down her leg, caressing her thigh until my hand met her boot. Tucking my fingers in the top of her boot, I used the leather in my grip to hook her leg more securely around my hips.

From here, I gave an experimental thrust, and another moan ripped from Charlotte, causing me to seal my mouth over hers. Her back rested against the top bar of the railing, keeping her secure between the metal and my body, but allowed the ridge my rock-solid cock created in my jeans to meet her denim-covered clit, just as I'd hoped. Charlotte squirmed again and again, her mouth moving against mine as her arms moved up to grip my biceps.

"Use me, Char. Take what you need," I muttered against her mouth. I wanted to pull my head back to watch this gorgeous woman use me for her pleasure, but I needed to swallow her noises, so we remained alone up here on this upper deck.

Charlotte set a quick pace with her hips, mine grinding to meet hers with every thrust.

"Fuck, don't stop," Charlotte whispered, her forehead pushed against mine, all her focus on her hip movements.

"I won't stop, but baby, you've gotta stay quiet. Can you do that for me?"

Charlotte nodded. "Harder, please."

I met her thrusts with everything I could, in some part of my mind aware that it was likely Charlotte would have a bruise across her back in the morning. My hand wandered up to palm her breast, under the vest but over her sweater, squeezing, hoping to brush her nipple through the layers of clothing. Successful or not, it seemed to tip her over the edge.

"I'm... I'm coming," Charlotte ground out, throwing her head back in a noiseless scream as her body lost all rhythm and convulsed against mine, her face absolutely gorgeous as she let go.

"Fuck," I ground out, burying my face in her shoulder to stop from yelling out as my own orgasm surprised me. Charlotte's ability to lose herself in her pleasure was too much for me.

We stood embracing, breathing heavily as our bodies calmed down when the five-minute warning for our arrival back at the Wharf sounded. I felt Charlotte's breathing normalize and then felt her shiver as her sweat dried and the air seemed even colder than it had been before.

"I'm going to need to carry that bag for you and not out of chivalry," I bit out, nodding at the bag that carried a scarf she had picked up during our Main Street wanderings.

Charlotte pushed me back slightly so she could see my face. "Wait, that voice sounds like one reserved for a guy with permanent blue balls. Did I misread the moment or did you not—"

"No, I did," I answered miserably. "Stupid cock. That was supposed to be about you."

Charlotte brought her hand to my face, looking into my eyes. "You have a very wet-pants situation going on right now because of me. Believe me, that memory will serve future Charlotte very well." A laugh erupted from her chest as she ended her sentence.

Her laughter was contagious, as I started laughing too, leaning down to give her a peck. "Future Hayden will keep future Charlotte very firmly in mind."

We felt the boat bump against the dock, as our bodies remained pressed together. I cleared my throat and stepped back, holding my hand out for the bag.

"So, a great day, right?" I said, as she straightened her clothes, ready to walk down the stairs in front of me.

"The best," she responded, though her smile seemed a bit sad before turning her back to me to grasp the railing and start her descent.

CHAPTER

Twenty

CHARLOTTE

Waking up on Sunday, I looked at my phone to see it was after 10:00 a.m. *There was that long sleep I was expecting.*

As I stretched in bed, I thought back to the night before, feeling my body heat at the memory of Hayden's body pressed against mine on the boat. I'd never had an orgasm in public before, let alone with my clothes on. *"Use me,"* I heard Hayden's voice say in that deep, growly voice that would narrate many future fantasies.

Remembering the distance that grew between us as we shared a car ride back to the apartment after leaving the boat cooled my temperature. My brain knew asking for space had been the right choice, even if my lady bits weren't currently speaking to me. My heart wasn't all that pleased, either.

I heard the water of Hayden's shower turn on across the hall, and I bolted up, knowing this was my chance to grab some coffee before hiding in my room the rest of the day. Not bothering with pants, I ran to the kitchen in an oversized T-shirt and my underwear, banking on the fact I could make it back behind a closed door before the shower turned off. Was avoiding Hayden the childish choice? Probably. But I needed a day of distance to cement my resolve, so I didn't melt into a puddle of desire at his feet.

As the coffee brewed, releasing the scent of hazelnut in the air, the liquid filled the largest mug we had in the condo. I raided the cupboards for all the snacks I could carry. I wanted to be fully prepared for a day of hermit mode. The telltale sound of the drip of coffee cutting off with a hiss signaled the cup was done brewing, and I picked it up by the handle while hugging the results of my snack foraging to my body. As I crossed the threshold to my room, I heard Hayden's bedroom door open, causing me to whip my body around to the back side of my door, pushing it closed with my hip.

Smooth, Charlotte.

I stood with my back pressed to my door, listening to the sounds of Hayden rummaging around in the kitchen. The sound of the blender whirred, confirming my suspicions he was in post-workout mode. I heard the rumble of the TV over the sound of the blender, the pre-NFL talking heads' voices mixing incoherently given the rest of the noise. Seems like Hayden wanted me to be very aware he would be posted up in the living room today, unlike yesterday's low-volume considerations.

Setting my coffee down on the nightstand and dumping the snacks into the middle of my bed, I climbed back in, propping pillows up against the headboard to create the perfect nest to spend the rest of the day in. I grabbed the romance I had brought home last night off the nightstand along with my coffee, taking a sip of the perfect brew, and opening to the first page, ready to dive into a witchy romantic world.

I had been successfully losing myself in fictional worlds for years, so I wasn't surprised when I looked up and noted the shadows in my room had changed. Checking my phone, I saw three hours had passed. I eyed both my empty water bottle and coffee mug, confirming the rumble of NFL Red Zone still continued on outside my room. My bladder would require a trip to the bathroom soon, and I should probably have some sort of protein, eyeing the empty bag of Twizzlers sitting next to me. Processed sugar and red dye do not make a balanced meal. I was just talking myself up to put on pants and reenter the rest of the apartment when my phone rang on the bed next to me.

"Mom" flashed on the caller ID, a picture of the two of us from my childhood in the bookstore appearing on the screen. It had been a few weeks since we had spoken, so I knew I needed to take the call. Maybe this conversation would be different. *Yeah, and Twizzlers don't have enough sugar to rot your teeth, Charlotte.*

"Hi, Mom," I answered, trying to effuse lightness into my voice.

"Hi there, Charlotte. How are you?"

"I'm doing all right. Got a nasty bout of the flu week before last, which was terrible timing with the gala being this past Friday, but I'm feeling a lot better and the gala was a huge success. So, all positive here."

"Oh, that was this weekend? Well, good."

I bit my lip as my stomach dropped. I know she hates that I'm here, but I'm positive I told her how important the gala was to me and how much work planning it was. Sharing how I had been enjoying the planning would have been a waste. She would have been insulted I could enjoy anything that wasn't working at our store.

"Yeah, it was this weekend. I'm really happy with the results. We raised a lot of funds and brought a ton of awareness to the Bookstore Future Fund."

"Well, you are in the big city. There are a lot of rich people there who need somewhere to throw their money. If you stroke their egos by calling a party a gala, it makes sense they would give something," she replied dismissively, making me regret I even tried connecting with her over this work. The fund had saved Ridge Reads after all, but that was a handout and my mother was too proud to admit she had needed one of those.

"How are things with you all? With the store?" Time to move this conversation along to the reason she called.

"Your Dad and I are fine. The store is fine. Will you be coming home for Thanksgiving?"

My mother, the most descriptive woman in the world, ladies and gentlemen.

"I don't think so, Mom. The tickets are going to be really expensive at this point and my internship is over two and a half weeks later, so I figured I'd just come home then."

"I would... We would like it if you could come home. Please," she reluctantly added.

I was taken aback. Was my mom getting sentimental about the holidays?

"Are you sure you and Dad are okay? I guess I would see about a tick—"

"Yes, your father and I are fine. We want to talk to you about your future regarding Ridge Reads."

My head fell back heavily against my headboard.

"My future with Ridge Reads," I said, not able to hide the defeated tone in my voice.

"Yes, given your internship will be over soon, we thought it would be a good time to talk about next steps. We've been talking to... it just seems like it's time."

"We've been over this. The internship could very well lead to a permanent job offer. And I'm going to be direct with you. It's an offer I would be very interested in accepting. I know you and Dad want me to take over Ridge Reads someday, but the work I'm doing here... it could help Ridge Reads and stores just like it all over the country. Do you not understand what that means to me?"

"I understand that you have a responsibility to this family and to *our* store."

"But what about what I *want*?" I whispered.

She didn't answer for a moment. I wondered if she'd heard me.

"We don't always get what we want, Charlotte. You're not a

child anymore. You should understand that. I hope we'll see you for Thanksgiving."

I didn't answer, not knowing what to say.

"Well, goodbye, Charlotte."

"Bye, Mom."

I sat with the phone in my hand, staring at nothing. I may not be a child anymore, but that conversation destroyed the childlike notion that there was anything I could do that would be acceptable to my parents outside of falling into line. I knew she hated I had left for this opportunity, but I thought if I could show her the good I could do with the IBA, she would come around. Instead, she wouldn't even listen to me long enough for me to make my case to her.

My bladder chose that moment to remind me it needed my attention, and I walked to the bathroom in a daze, no longer giving weight to whether Hayden would be waiting for me when I exited. Going through the motions, I sat there, my head in my hands, not sure where to go from here. Existential dread on the toilet. This had to be a new low.

Getting up to wash my hands, I looked at myself in the mirror. Looking back at me was the girl I had always known—blond hair, button nose, round cheeks. It was her eyes that looked different to me now. They looked lost, unsure what to do next. I truly believed I could do more for the book world with an organization like the IBA than I could running a small-town bookstore. But could I live knowing that may irrevocably break something between my parents and me? Did it have to be my happiness or theirs? Denying myself what I had been working toward, what I wanted?

A cheer trickled in from the living room, the sound of Hayden's exuberance over some football play or another. Hayden. He represented another chance to live for myself, to make myself happy. And I was denying that for what, to focus on an internship that I already loved, was already good at, and was already over-dedicated to? Was I shoving myself into an emotional small-town box by not experiencing what Hayden had to offer, what we could be together?

I saw the eyes of the girl in the mirror morph from sadness to determination. If being in DC was all about doing things for myself, then that was going to include doing the handsome man on the other side of the bathroom wall.

I stalked out of the bathroom, headed toward the living room. Hayden's broad shoulders were wrapped in a tight T-shirt visible over the back of the couch. I came to stand in front of the chaise part of the sectional, my eyes taking in the way Hayden's threadbare blue shirt clung to chest as well. He wore tight grey joggers again, because apparently, he couldn't wear anything else but the sexy man-pant uniform around the house.

"Charlotte?" Hayden asked while his eyes traveled from my feet, up over my bare legs, pausing at the line where my long T-shirt stopped at the top of my thighs, before traveling up to meet my eyes.

"This an important game?" I asked, my eyes back on his crotch, where his dick was making itself noticeable against his right thigh. *Blessed joggers.*

"Well, I mean it's Red Zone, so it's not just one game but—"

"Perfect," I said, crossing the last few feet between us and lowering myself until I straddled his lap then crashing my mouth to his.

Hayden sat still for a few seconds, just long enough for me to panic that perhaps my pouncing was too aggressive, before he let out a delicious groan into my mouth. He wrapped his arms around my waist and met the strokes of my lips. Opening for me without any prompting, the kiss deepened and I felt our teeth clink with the fervor of our kiss.

Hayden pulled back.

"Whoa, wait. Charlotte, are you okay?"

"I'm fine," I said, trying to get his mouth back on mine.

"But did something happen? Last night, you were steadfast that this... we couldn't happen."

If he was determined to use his mouth for talking, I'd take my lip's talents elsewhere. I started kissing the side of his neck, headed toward his ear, finding a spot behind it that made his hips hitch up when I licked it.

"That was last night. This is now," I said as I continued my trail of kisses down his neck, across his throat and up the other side.

"This is now..." Hayden groaned, tilting his head to give me more access to his throat, which I gladly lavished with attention.

Bringing my mouth back to his, he kissed me passionately for a moment before pulling back again and putting his hands on my arms, holding me still, shaking his head.

"Okay, Charlotte, seriously. Something had to happen."

I blew out a heavy breath, feeling some hairs that had crossed in front of my face during my ministrations lift with the air.

"I just talked to my mom."

"Sexy," Hayden said, smirking at me, but his eyes held a look of concern.

I laughed in spite of the heaviness of the conversation.

"She just made it very clear that no matter what I did here, the only thing she expects from me is to fall in line and come back home. I'm not sure I'll ever find a solution that makes us both happy, so I decided I wanted to chase happiness here. While I can."

"So she wants you to go home and work at the store after the internship is over?"

"Yup. All she wanted to do was talk about me coming home for Thanksgiving."

"Oh, you're going home for Thanksgiving? My family is coming to DC, I was hoping you might—"

I moved forward to kiss this amazing, wonderful man, who might be too good to be true.

"Charlotte, wait."

I leaned back, his tone imploring me to cool my lady bits and listen to him.

"My cock wants to end me for saying this, but I don't want you to fuck me, to be with me out of spite. I want you to want to do this for you."

"I do want it for me. I want it for us. I'm tired of denying myself of the things I want, the things that could be good for me, just because they scare me. I can have more than just one good thing in my life."

I felt like I could see fireworks going off in Hayden's eyes as the largest smile I had ever seen crossed his face. He pulled my head toward him, his lips still smiling as they moved against mine, my mouth curling up in answer.

CHAPTER

Twenty-One

HAYDEN

The feeling of Charlotte on my lap, pushing me into the couch in broad daylight, did something to my insides. I felt like I could float along the ceiling, but also had never felt more grounded than when I had the chance to hold this woman. We were a perfect fit. My hands explored her body, skimming up her bare legs to meet the cotton of her shirt at her hips.

"I should have known you were trouble when you came out dressed like this," I muttered, nipping at Charlotte's chin while she ground her hips in my lap.

"What can I say? I'm a master of seduction when I'm having an existential crisis and earth-shattering breakthrough in the same moment." She tilted her head, encouraging me to explore her neck. I pulled down the collar of her shirt, much like I had with her sweater last night, but the stretch of the material gave much better access to her collarbone. I lavished kisses there, biting down lightly, wanting to leave my mark somehow. Seeing the red bloom on her fair skin immediately made my dick harder, which I thought was impossible at this point.

My hands moved around her back, sliding under her T-shirt

and down past the waistband of her underwear. My hands rested there, enjoying the fullness of Charlotte's ass.

Well, this is just where my hands live now. It will be hard to get work done, but sacrifices had to be made.

Charlotte moved her hands to the hem of my shirt, her fingers tickling along my abs. She groaned. "I've wanted to pet these since the day you moved in."

I shuddered under her touch. "They aren't complaining." I leaned back into the couch cushion to give her unrestricted access. She responded by widening her thighs so she could push my shirt up, forcing me to remove my hands from their new happy place so she could lift it over my head.

Charlotte sat back for a moment, taking me in, and I felt oddly on display. It wasn't the first time Charlotte had seen my chest, but it was the first time she'd seen it like this.

"God, you're beautiful," she murmured before leaning forward to kiss me again, guiding my hands back to her ass.

I felt my chest warm. I knew I wasn't unattractive, but I'm not sure I've ever been called beautiful. Hot, maybe, which made me feel more like a piece of meat than a man. Beautiful made me feel cherished, *seen*.

Charlotte's fingers tangled in my hair, tugging so I was angled for her to work from her position above me. Gosh, kissing was great. I could do this fore—

"Do you have any condoms?" Charlotte leaned back to look at my face.

My dick twitched. Right, kissing was great, but sex was pretty awesome too.

I felt my face fall. "I don't. I realized my ex didn't pack them when she kicked me out and I... I haven't had a reason to buy any more since then."

Charlotte smiled sweetly at me, seeming to understand I hadn't let myself dream we'd get here.

"I don't either, but I do have an IUD, and my last test results were negative. I got a physical before I moved here."

"My last results were negative too. I don't think Veronica cheated on me, but considering she kicked me out on the advice of her new psychic, I decided I better be sure."

Charlotte giggled. "Different strokes for different folks, but I'm still not over that's why she kicked you out."

I tickled her sides. "Glad you can laugh at my pain."

Charlotte laughed fully as she squirmed when my fingers found a vulnerable spot. My dick was confused. Charlotte was still on top of me, the warmth of her center reaching through the fabric of my sweatpants, but she was laughing. We both were, and that wasn't something I had ever had during sex before. This communication and bantering and laughter. It was new.

Charlotte trapped my hands, pushing them over my head, curling my fingers so they wrapped around the back of the couch. She pushed herself up on her knees so my chin was nestled between her breasts. Looking down, she said, "But you can take a little pain, can't you?"

"Huh?"

"Stay just like this, please."

I nodded as Charlotte slid off my lap and kneeled between my legs on the floor. She put the warm heat of her tongue to the tip of my cock—still in the joggers—the grey color of the fabric darkening. I felt my slit leaking, adding to the dampness.

"I'd really rather not come in my pants two days in a row."

I felt the vibration of Charlotte's laugh against my cock and groaned.

"I suppose that's reasonable. Here, lift up."

I lifted my hips as Charlotte grasped the waistband and brought them down to my knees. My cock sprang free, standing in salute to the gorgeous blond on the floor before me.

Charlotte eyed my cock with hunger. "Well, that explains last night. You're working with a real lightsaber in your pants, to work through two layers of denim."

"I'm not sure why I'm surprised that works for me, but it does. Please wield my lightsaber, baby."

Charlotte laughed. "Nope, you ruined it. But you'll still get what you want."

She leaned forward, circling her tongue around the tip, dipping into the slit, and lapping up the beads of pre-cum. She took my entire cock in her mouth, as far as she could go, before releasing me and bringing her hand up to stroke my cock. Her grip was just a hair too light, and meeting her eyes, I realized she was very aware.

"Something you'd like, Hayden?"

"Your mouth, your hand, firmer. I'm not picky."

"My favorite—dealer's choice."

Charlotte bent back down over my cock, swallowing as much as she could, her hand covering the rest, covering me from root to tip. She bobbed up and down in a steady rhythm, and I felt my balls start to tighten already. Her other hand came up to palm them, and my hips started to thrust. My hand came down to rest on the top of her head.

She stopped suddenly.

"Wha—"

"Hands on the couch, please and thank you."

I growled as I removed my hand from her head and returned it to gripping the fabric. I was going to owe Duncan a new couch if I wasn't careful.

She returned to her work, adding in a swirl of her tongue around the tip after every third stroke. The familiar tingling in my balls returned and again, my hips thrusted gently in time with the strokes of her mouth. I felt my balls draw up and then—

Charlotte licked her lips, her mouth no longer around my dick, her fingers squeezing at the base.

"Fuck!"

"Something wrong?"

"Nope, just peachy," I gritted out, recognizing Charlotte wanted me to beg to finish.

"Perfect." Charlotte smiled wickedly before running her tongue from the base of my cock to the tip. A groan left my chest, with no chance of restraining it. Her mouth moved down to my balls, taking one, then the other in her mouth, her fingers running feather light up my thighs and across my pelvis, but avoiding my leaking cock.

"Mmmpf," I said, past the point of forming words.

Charlotte looked up at me, her fingers continuing their trail of torture.

Something in her blue eyes, promising wickedness and affection at the same time, broke me.

"Charlotte, please, can I come?"

"Hmmm, we'll see."

She returned her mouth to my cock, hollowing her cheeks and taking me in further than before. I felt the tip enter the tightness of her throat. Her hand returned to my balls, handling them with the perfect touch. I tried to keep my hips still this time, taking away the tell that I was about to finish, but Charlotte pulled her mouth off just before I unloaded, anyway.

I threw my arm over my eyes as I groaned, hoping that it being in the near-my-head region would comply with Charlotte's rules.

"Hayden," her voice said gently.

"Yes?" I ground out.

"Release your hands. Touch me, please."

I removed my arm from my face to look down at her, her hand wrapped around the bottom of my cock, mouth hovering just above it, waiting for me to show her what I needed.

I wrapped my hands in her hair and thrust up into her waiting mouth, still aware I was a lot to take. Her hand grasped my hip, the pressure and her eye contact encouraged me to push further. I started to fuck her mouth in earnest, her eyes watering, but taking me to the back of her throat like a dream. I felt the familiar tingles for the fourth time and almost felt afraid of the feeling. I wasn't sure I could survive coming back from the edge one more time. But Charlotte didn't pull off. Instead, she tightened her grip on my hips as she continued to take me down.

"Charlotte, I'm—"

And that's all I got before I shot everything I had down her throat. It may have been the longest orgasm of my life, thanks to the beautiful torture she put me through.

I released her hair, sunk into the couch, boneless, as I tried to catch my breath. Charlotte smiled up at me, wiping a bit of liquid from the corner of her mouth, a bit of my load trying to escape.

"Get on up here," I said, opening my arms to welcome her against my chest. The brush of the fabric of her shirt against my skin shot through my heightened senses, as I brought her face to mine for a gentle kiss.

"Hated the process, but loved the result," I said when I pulled away after a while.

Charlotte shrugged. "It felt right in the moment. But I guess it's okay we don't have a condom."

My body took that as a challenge, my energy returning after Charlotte had sucked it out of my dick.

"Why do you say that?" I asked, gripping the bottom of Charlotte's shirt and pushing it over her head, revealing her bare chest. My hands drifted up to brush the bottom of her breasts, causing her to shiver. "I think I'll just have to lay you back on this couch and eat you until he's ready to go again. Which given how good your skin feels against my hands and how amazing I've dreamed you taste, shouldn't be long at all. But don't worry, I'll put up a good showing, regardless. Then, let's see if people on the street can hear you scream while I fuck you. It's fifteen stories—a real challenge."

Charlotte looked at me wide-eyed, her chest quickly rising—

up and down—as she nodded. "That sounds like an acceptable way to spend a Sunday afternoon."

I laughed, easing her off my lap and pushing her down like I said I would.

"It sounds practically perfect to me."

Text Interlude

AUSTIN, BLAIRE, AND CHARLOTTE GROUP CHAT

AUSTIN (4:17 PM)

Charlie Brown, why have you ignored my calls and texts all weekend? How did the gala go? I've brought in the big guns to be sure we have confirmation of life.

BLAIRE (4:20 PM)

Austin, I told you, she thumbs upped my good luck text after the gala was over. She's alive, just recovering.

AUSTIN (4:22 PM)

A kidnapper could have done that. I don't trust it.

BLAIRE (4:25 PM)

Have you been watching true crime documentaries again?

AUSTIN (4:26 PM)

Only as a palette cleanser from my podcasts.

BLAIRE (4:28 PM)

You and Cole and those podcasts, ridiculous - no one is coming to murder you.

AUSTIN (4:29 PM)

That's what all those victims thought too…

CHARLOTTE (4:30 PM)

Do you actually need me for any of this?

AUSTIN (4:31 PM)

LOTTIE LOU - prove to us it's actually you.

CHARLOTTE (4:33 PM):

You're ridiculous.

BLAIRE (4:34 PM)

You know he won't stop until you do…

CHARLOTTE (4:36 PM)

The gala went really well, and it's been a busy weekend. I went to visit a bookstore yesterday, and today was just a day relaxing in bed.

AUSTIN (4:38 PM)

Anyone with access to the internet would know those are your favorite weekend activities. Doesn't cut it.

CHARLOTTE (4:42 PM)

Impossible boy whom I love very much… Okay, fine. Hayden and I may have… consummated our roommateship today, after spending the day together yesterday.

BLAIRE (4:43 PM)

David Rose Excuse Me.gif

AUSTIN (4:45 PM)

FUCK YES. I've been waiting for this message. Tell me everything.

BLAIRE (4:46 PM)

Ignore him. You do not have to do that.

AUSTIN (4:48 PM)

I'm hearing about someone's sex life in this group chat. It'll distract me from the fact I'm not getting any. So, Blaire, wanna tell me why you and Cole had Christmas lights lying on his nightstand in October instead?

BLAIRE (4:49 PM)

Charlotte, for the love of God, please take one for the team here.

CHARLOTTE (4:53 PM)

Can't, sorry. Hayden's sitting right here and says if I'm using the phrase "consummated our roommateship," he didn't do it right. So byeeeeee. *wave emoji*

AUSTIN (4:54 PM)

You lucky bitch!

AUSTIN (4:57 PM)

So, Blaire...

Blaire Greene has notifications silenced

CHAPTER
Twenty~Two

HAYDEN

I felt like humming as I entered my office might be a little unnecessary, on top of the huge smile and spring in my step, but it was an effort to restrain myself. I'm sure other great weekends had occurred in my past, but nothing was coming to mind that even came close to this past one. Waking up with Charlotte in my bed this morning, being able to kiss her when I felt like—life was good. We hadn't talked about where things were headed or what this meant for the future. For once in my life, I was trying to enjoy the hand I was dealt instead of trying to plan three moves ahead.

"Good morning, Hayden," Leslie greeted me, an amused smirk on her face. Fuck, I had been humming after all, hadn't I? Oh well, it was a great day.

"Good morning, Leslie. Happy Monday!"

"Good weekend, was it then? You had a good time at the gala?"

"It was the perfect weekend. The gala was just the start. Do you mind sending me the number for a good florist? I want to surprise someone with a bouquet today."

"Oh, of course. Absolutely. You know, I could do that for you.

I'm sure you have other things to attend to," Leslie said uncertainly.

"And you would do a splendid job picking them out, but this is one flower order I'd like to handle myself. Maybe I'll even go down to a shop at lunch and pick something out in person."

Leslie was attempting to contain laughter at this point. "Must be a very special someone."

"You don't miss a beat, Leslie," I said with a wink.

I couldn't care less if she was making fun of me a bit. I probably deserved it for the obnoxious mood I was in. "I'll see you in thirty minutes with that florist information and to go over my schedule for the week?"

"You got it, Hayden. I'll be in then."

I switched to whistling as I entered my office, taking off my suit jacket and hanging it on the back of my chair. I had just wiggled my mouse, waking my computer from its weekend slumber, when my phone rang.

"Hayden, Preston's on the phone for you. Do you want me to put him through?"

"Oh, go ahead. These emails will keep for a few minutes longer."

Leslie's snort echoed from the handset and through the open door in stereo.

"I'll patch him right through, then."

I tapped my pen on my desk, waiting for the call to connect.

"Hey there, Hayden. How was the rest of your weekend?"

"It was spectacular, big bro. How are you on this fine Monday?"

Preston laughed at me.

"Someone got laid this weekend,"

"Now, now, big brother, do you talk to the senator with that mouth? You know a gentleman doesn't kiss and tell... multiple times."

"Gross. Your cheery attitude is souring my coffee."

"Well, you know you could try going out and meeting someone on your own, Prez."

Preston laughed. "Yeah, maybe once we win reelection, I'll have time to think about getting a life. Speaking of which, I have to get to a strategy session, but I wanted to see if you wanted to do lunch this week? I recall owing you from the gala on Friday."

"Yeah, man, that would be great. How's Wednesday for you?"

There was a pause while Preston consulted his overstuffed calendar.

"Wednesday would be great. I'll make a reservation somewhere and let you know?"

"Sounds good." I thought for a moment. "Actually, want to make it a dinner instead of lunch and have that reservation be for three? If Charlotte can't make it, I'll let you know, but I'd love for you to have a real chance to get to know her."

"Wow! You're serious about this girl, aren't you?"

I smiled, thinking about the way Charlotte's eyes opened and a smile crossed her face when she saw me next to her this morning. Like waking up to see me first thing was just as great for her as it was for me.

"I'm seriously happy right now, and that's enough for me. So, reservation for the three on Wednesday?"

"You got it. I'll text you later with the details. Try not to make anyone else throw up today."

"I make no promises. Have a good Monday, big bro."

I hung up the handset and picked up my cell phone. Was it too obvious to text her about dinner with Preston now, considering I had just dropped her off at work less than an hour ago?

Deciding I wasn't about to start playing games now, I typed out a message, asking her if she'd be free for dinner with my brother. Everyone could make fun of me all day, every day. As long as I had her, I was playing for keeps.

The first half of the week passed in a blur of long days of work, followed by nights that felt so quick by comparison. Now that we had given into the chemistry between us, simple acts like watching TV on the couch easily turned into contests of who could ignore heavy petting over—and under—clothes the longest until I had Charlotte bent over the arm of the couch or she rode me on the floor. I had the lack of sleep and rug burns to prove it, but I never felt happier.

As we exited the Metro to meet Preston for a late dinner at a dim sum place in Chinatown, Charlotte fell uncharacteristically quiet beside me.

"Everything okay, Char?"

"Hmm? Oh yeah, everything's fine," she answered, fidgeting with the strap of her purse crossed over her shoulder.

More silence continued as we crossed the street.

"Are you sure?"

"You're going to think I'm silly."

"Try me," I said, grabbing her hand away from her purse strap and interlacing her fingers with mine.

Charlotte smiled down at our joined hands.

"I'm just nervous. I want Preston to like me. I know how important your brothers are to you."

"Nah, just Hunter, and he likes everyone. I don't care what Preston thinks."

"Hayden..."

"I promise he's going to like you, because he knows I like you. And besides, what's not to like? Beautiful, smart, funny. Really. I would be worried about him trying to steal you away if he wasn't a complete and total workaholic. Plus, that whole bro-code thing."

Charlotte laughed, her shoulders lowering from her ears slightly. I consider my mission accomplished, just in time for us to reach the restaurant.

"So, you like me, huh?" Charlotte said, her eyes twinkling as she walked in front of me while I held the door.

I crowded behind her in the vestibule while she waited for the people exiting the restaurant to pass, leaning close to her ear.

"I hope the orgasm I gave you on the kitchen island before we left would confirm that, but if it wasn't enough, I'm happy to show you again tonight... twice."

Charlotte's breath hitched, turning her head to look at me, her cheeks an appealing pink, which I was learning was a mixture of desire and embarrassment of hearing me talk like this in public.

My mouth moved toward hers when movement through the glass door in front of us caught my eye, and I saw Preston standing, watching us. His arms folded, his head shaking, but with a smile on his face, in good humor.

"Later," I said, stepping back so I could move around Charlotte and grab the interior door for her. "Our dinner date is waiting." I nodded toward Preston so she would spot him, too.

Charlotte's cheeks darkened even more as she moved through the door toward my brother.

"Charlotte, I presume," Preston greeted her, holding out his hand.

Charlotte reached out. "It's nice to meet you, Preston. I'm sorry your brother has no manners and didn't manage to introduce us at the gala last Friday."

Preston barked out a laugh, and I felt my grin widen. *That's my girl.*

"Well, ya know, we did the best we could with him, but some street dogs just can't be taught manners."

"Funny," Charlotte pursed her lips. "Hayden told me a story about you insulting a foreign dignitary from the Philippines by beckoning one of their staff to come talk to you by curling your finger? Doesn't sound like good manners to me."

It was my time to laugh loudly. Preston lifted his hands to give Charlotte a light applause for a well-landed barb.

"Let's get some food and drinks before we go any more rounds. I can tell I'm going to need my wits about me. Shall we?"

Preston extended his arm, and Charlotte laced hers through his elbow without hesitation, throwing a smile at me over her shoulder as they made their way to the hostess stand to be seated.

Dinner passed without much incident. Charlotte asked Preston a lot of questions about his work for the senator, showing real interest in his answers. They discovered a shared love of audiobooks and discussed some of their favorite narrators.

The waiter came by to collect our empty baskets, leaving us with a dessert menu and the rest of our drinks.

"So," Preston started. "How exactly did this happen? Hayden was very insistent on using words like friendship and roommate on Friday night, but that is clearly no longer your vibe."

Charlotte looked at me. "I'm not really sure how to explain it..."

"Well, my leg hair growing back certainly did help," I said, winking at Charlotte.

"We've been over this. You came into my room first. You asked for it."

"Only because you triple-pranked me before 8:00 a.m."

"The kitchen faucet sprayer is a classic, Charlotte. I'm saving that one for Christmas morning. At least three brothers usually have a hangover after too much eggnog and whisky the night before. It'll be perfect," Preston said.

"Oh, you tattled on me to your brother, huh?" Charlotte said, crossing her arms and turning her body toward me.

"I did no such thing. My twin is a loudmouth," I responded.

Preston nodded. "He is, and Duncan is a gossip, too. He called me as soon as you got done pitching the gala table sponsorship, telling me I had to make sure I got a seat at that table so I could report back."

Charlotte laughed. "I'm an only child, so I'm way out of my element with this sibling thing. But, to answer your original question, that's probably what sealed the deal on *this* happening."

Preston nodded. "Helpful when you have biggest brother's company's money to bail you out of a prank gone too far."

I winced.

Charlotte touched my hand. "I may have been a bit high-strung about the whole text debacle. Yes, it was an absolutely *terrible* decision on Hayden's part to put my real name and work phone number on the internet, but there were a lot of background factors about work and my family situation Hayden had no way of knowing. And he's more than made up for it between taking care of me when I had the flu and making sure I could stay home and rest by saving the gala."

I flipped my hand over to grasp hers.

Preston looked between us in that analytical way of his. He nodded, seeming to approve of something in his own head.

"Well, I'm glad Hayden helped you loosen up," he lobbied, taking a final sip of his drink, ice clanking, while raising an eyebrow at the two of us.

Charlotte blushed and covered her face.

"Sorry, Charlotte, I'm just trying to prepare you for Thanksgiving. Four brothers, one father, one stepmother, maybe a video call from brother number five. I promise I'm the gentle giant of the group."

Charlotte looked over at me.

Preston grimaced. "He has invited you to Thanksgiving at my place, right?"

I glared daggers at my brother. "No more drinks for you tonight, Prez. Charlotte, I mentioned it in passing, but most of my family will be at Preston's for Thanksgiving. Do you want to join us? I know your parents want you to come home..."

"Tell you what," Preston butted in. "Come to my place Friday for trick-or-treating on Capitol Hill. There will be candy and lots of cute kids in costumes. And this way, we both just invited you to a holiday to make it less awkward my brother just only offi-cially invited you to Thanksgiving in front of me."

Charlotte laughed. "I'm in for both. I can't think of anywhere I'd rather be," she finished, looking over at me with a warm smile.

I wrapped my arm around the back of her chair as the conversation between the three of us continued. Perhaps living in the city wasn't so bad after all, if it led to evenings like this.

CHAPTER
Twenty~Three

CHARLOTTE

Thanksgivings in years past had been spent in a darkened bookstore, organizing for a big weekend of sales ahead of the official start of the holiday shopping season. Our store, like many others in downtown Holly Ridge, benefited massively from the huge Christmas festival the town threw each year. Over the years, my parents mastered what those traveling from out of town were looking for from sales on those days. Locals dropped in on weekdays throughout December for their gift needs, avoiding the major crowds.

When I was younger, I loved those days spent with my parents in the dark, sorting and organizing. My mom would run home every hour to check on the turkey cooking in the oven, somehow never burning the house down while we left it to brown on its own. We would come back to an aromatic and cozy homestead, rushing around to throw together sides and set the table, starving after a hard day's work of physical labor. In possibly predictable niche fashion, we would go around saying what books we were thankful had been published that year, feeling the undercurrent of gratefulness for our family and our small-town buzz around the room. Then it would be early to bed after we did the dishes, a seamless team in sync with each other.

I can't pinpoint exactly when I fell out of sync with the rest of my team, but the first pandemic Thanksgiving really brought it home. We sat around staring at each other throughout the entire day that Thursday, not sure what to expect for a holiday shopping weekend when we could only have five people in the store at a time to maintain safe distancing for ourselves and our shoppers. I had been pushing my parents all year to upgrade our systems and invest in a website, but our numbers were just too tight for them to justify something that scared them. I felt like I was on the outside looking in, screaming through a window, just to find the glass was too thick to be heard.

It was these Thanksgivings past I was thinking of while I stood at the stove in my Washington DC condo, stirring cranberries soaking in mulled wine and watching potato chunks bubbling in boiling water. My boyfriend-type person sat on the couch, calling out anytime there was something in the Macy's Thanksgiving Day Parade he thought I would want to see. The first few weeks of November had passed by in rainy days, couch cuddles, too many *Star Wars* movies, and okay, an insane amount of sex. The playful, yet passionate nature of our relationship was something I'd never experienced before, but was quickly becoming addicted to. I blushed, thinking back to last night when Hayden asked about the Thanksgiving-themed smut I was reading on my e-reader, a book about a creature with the powers to grant wishes through sexual completion with another person. Hayden offered to see if this was a power he had developed over the past few hours, and well, if my wish was three orgasms in a row, then I think the experiment was a success.

"Hmm, I love these pink cheeks. Thinking of me?" Hayden came up behind me, wrapping his arms around my waist.

"Nah, just heat from the stove," I teased, leaning back into him.

"Liar," he whispered into my ear, planting a quick kiss on my cheek before letting go and leaning his back against the counter next to me.

"What are you thinking about over here? I tried to get your attention so you could see the Snoopy balloon, my personal favorite, but you were in your own little world."

"Oh shoot. Sorry, just... thinking about how different this Thanksgiving is from Thanksgivings past. You know, this is the first time I've spent it away from my parents, away from the store?"

Hayden nodded solemnly. "I assumed it might be, with how important the days following are for retail stores."

"I'm so happy to be spending it with you and I'm excited—and nervous—to spend it with your family. I just didn't expect to feel so conflicted about not spending it with my own family."

"Well, you should definitely give them a call. Wish them a Happy Thanksgiving."

I nodded. "I will, I will. The cranberries are almost done and the potatoes will need mashing here soon..."

"Char, are you avoiding your parents?"

I tore my eyes away from the stove, where they had been proving a watched pot can boil sometimes, and met Hayden's gaze.

"Not consciously, at least until today, but I think I am. I just like our little bubble, you know? And talking to them is going to force a conversation about the future, which forces a conversation about *our* future, and I just wasn't ready."

Hayden stepped forward, turning my body away from the stove and into his. His eyes were inches from mine. "I've liked the bubble too, but ignoring the outside world won't stop it from crashing the party. And personally, I'd like to take on the outside world with you. We can figure out the rest as it comes."

I closed my eyes, putting my forehead on his chest, breathing in a smell that was just entirely Hayden—woody, clean, and safe. "I'd like that too," I mumbled into the grey fabric of his T-shirt.

Hayden laughed, gripping my chin and tilting it up so my

mouth was no longer smooshed against his body. "What was that now?"

"I'd like that too," I said softly, not able to look away from the magnetic powers of his gaze.

He lowered his mouth to mine for a soft kiss, lifting away after a moment. My mouth tried to chase his, but he held me firmly in place.

He reached around and smacked my ass, causing me to yelp, breaking the serious atmosphere that had settled over the kitchen. As usual, Hayden knew just what I needed.

"All right then. Let's get this food finished, watch Santa cross into Herald Square, and get ourselves over to Preston's before Hunter eats all the good hors d'oeuvres."

A couple of hours later, Preston was guiding Hayden and me into a massive club room on the top floor of his apartment building.

As I handed Hayden our dinner contributions to take off my coat, I said to Preston, "You know, when you said you were hosting Thanksgiving at your place, this is not at all what I had in mind."

Preston snorted. "Can you imagine fitting four Brandt brothers, plus you, Dad, and Margaret into my studio downstairs? Duncan ponied up the money to rent this space for the day, I think out of guilt since he's not able to make it back to the States until next week. I had to trade political favors to steal the space away from the chief of staff for the Speaker of the House. Welcome to a very DC Thanksgiving, Charlotte."

I laughed as Preston took my coat from me and directed Hayden where to take our dishes in the full kitchen the space boasted to the right of the door. Standing alone in the middle of the room, I took in the huge windows, offering a view of a sun-drenched Capitol and Congress's office buildings. Shouts coming from my left, where a large screen TV was surrounded by brown leather couches and armchairs, quickly distracted me from the view. I could see the back of two male heads, sporting brown hair similar in color to Hayden's, seated and watching a football game. Looking at the screen, it seemed someone had just scored a touchdown.

Hayden appeared at my side and steered me toward the couches and his brothers.

"Hey, dickheads, can we keep the shouting to a minimum, at least until a real football team plays?"

A face almost identical to Hayden's on the surface turned around to face us. "Spencer's being a sore loser because I'm playing him in fantasy this week, and Hendricks has already scored two touchdowns in the first quarter."

"Maybe I wouldn't be a sore loser if you weren't a gloating asshole about it. Ever think about that?" the youngest Brandt brother countered, pulling his eyes away from the screen to face us as well.

"Charlotte, these animals are my brothers, Spencer and Hunter. I'd apologize for them, but you've seen me watch football, so you get it."

I smiled at them, hoping my nerves didn't show. "I learned early on that suggesting players should get extra points for how good they looked in their football pants was a good way to almost see Hayden's head explode. I'm happy to share my point value system with you, if you're interested."

Hayden rolled his eyes as his brothers laughed.

Hunter extended his hand over the back of the couch to shake mine, his button-down shirt sleeves rolled up to reveal colorful full-sleeve tattoos on both arms. Upon closer inspection, he shared facial features with Hayden, but there was a tiredness around his eyes that Hayden didn't have.

"Charlotte, good to meet you. Hayden has been annoyingly mum on the details, so thanks for hanging out with Preston so we could at least know a few things about you."

"You're such a fucking gossip, Hunt. Hi, Charlotte, I'm Spencer. I don't gossip with my brothers, so I know nothing about you. Want to play twenty questions later?"

"Psh, you don't gossip? Then, please tell me how his entire grade knew that Hayden had made it to second base under the bleachers with Natalie Menendez moments after it happened?" Preston asked, coming up to join our little group.

"Okay, okay. I don't gossip about my brothers *anymore*," the baby of the family relented, as the others laughed, clearly unashamed of his past crimes.

"Natalie, under the bleachers, hmm," I teased, looking over at Hayden.

"All right, I need a beer. Anyone else?" Hayden asked, heading over to the fridge.

"Me, please," Hunter and Spencer said in unison.

"Not yet for me," Preston answered, holding his beer over his head, eyes glued to the game on the TV.

Hayden looked back and made eye contact with me as I shook my head. I felt like I needed my full wits about me for a bit longer.

Hayden returned with bottles for himself, Hunter, and Spencer. He took a draw from the long neck, then asked, "So, where are Dad and Margaret?"

"They're down in my apartment watching over Margaret's pies. Fewer ingredients to lug up here that way."

Hayden nodded. "Makes sense. So, football?" He looked over at me, gesturing with his head to the empty love seat perpendicular to the TV.

"As long as Preston doesn't need help with anything for the food?" I answered, looking over at the chef in question.

"Thank you for displaying manners my brothers lack, but we're in the calm before the storm now. I might even be able to sit for a bit myself," Preston said as he waved me over to join Hayden on the love seat.

"Besides, I wouldn't want to miss twenty questions during

the commercial breaks," he continued, settling into one of the recliners.

"He wasn't kidding about twenty questions?" I muttered to Hayden.

"Oh, Spencer never jokes about car games," Hayden answered. "Even when there's a car nowhere near us."

"Damn right. Undefeated license plate game champion," Spencer said, looking over at us. "But you may want to get a beer. The penalty for skipping a question is having to take a drink. Brandt house rules."

"We'll share," Hayden answered, putting his arm around my shoulder and giving it a squeeze.

Spencer tipped his beer in acknowledgment. Thirty seconds of comfortable silence passed until a game break appeared and Spencer turned his full attention to me, a charismatic smile spreading across his face.

"Okay, Charlotte. Tell me, what is, in your opinion, my brother's most annoying habit?"

"Well," I started, Hayden looking over at me, seeming shocked I had such a quick answer. "I definitely don't like it when Preston fishes ice out of his drinks to chew on."

All the brothers laughed, including Preston, who shot me a wink at my clever response.

Spencer clinked the neck of his beer bottle with mine. "Well played, Charlotte. I'll have to keep my eye on you. One question down, nineteen to go."

I nestled closer to Hayden's side, enjoying the brothers' bickering and football commentary. It was nothing like a Thanksgiving I had ever known, but it turned out, change could be a good thing.

Two quarters of football later, we were on question seventeen when the door to the club room opened. An older man with Brandt-brown hair and broad shoulders held the door open with one hand and balanced a pie on an oven mitt in his other hand. Passing through the open door was an older woman with chin-length grey hair, carrying a pie in each hand.

"Pies are here," the woman announced, carrying the day's desserts over to the island in the kitchen area. "Preston, it smells just wonderful in here," she said as Preston closed the oven door, checking on the turkey. He straightened up to accept a kiss on the cheek, squeezing the woman's shoulder with affection.

Hayden stood up and held his hand out to help me out of the sunken love seat. Taking my hand in his, we walked over to join the group in the kitchen.

"Hayden!" the woman exclaimed as we reached them, wrapping him in a hug that he dropped my hand to return. "Charlotte," she said to me, after letting him go, holding her arms out. "Is a hug hello, okay?"

"Sure," I answered, stepping into her arms and circling mine loosely around her back. She ended the hug quickly.

"Charlotte, I believe you know this hugger, my stepmom, Margaret Hayes."

"Oh, you," Margaret waved her hands at Hayden. "I'd blame the bottle of wine we opened while making pies, but he's right. I am a hugger. We're so happy you were able to join us today. It's so lovely to see you in an atmosphere outside the bookstore. I'll try to avoid asking you about books for the *whole* day."

"I'm not sure I get through a single conversation without mentioning a book, so maybe it should be a goal for us both," I smiled back, instantly feeling at ease in her presence. "Thank you again for connecting me with Duncan through my mom. My class schedule last summer didn't allow me to be at the store regularly on Tuesday mornings when you came in for your new releases, so I hadn't seen you in person to thank you. But being able to stay at his place has been amazing."

I heard a snort from the peanut gallery behind me. Maybe amazing wasn't the best word to use when I was here as her stepson's date.

Margaret smiled indulgently. "I was going to be sure Hayden checked in with you a few times while you were in town, but seems like fate and Duncan's old assistant had something else in mind. Feels like a good match to me."

Hayden's cheeks turned slightly pink at Margaret's exuberance. "And this quiet giant back here is my dad, Stephen."

"Hi, Charlotte. I hope my boys haven't been too hard on you this afternoon. We're glad you're here."

"Thank you, Stephen."

"Good to see you, Dad," Hayden said, wrapping his arms around his dad in a hug that was enthusiastically returned, back slaps and all.

"All right, so where are we? What needs to be done next?"

Hunter called from the other side of the room, "Charlotte still has three more questions to answer."

"Twenty questions?" Stephen asked knowingly, the affection for his sons apparent in the pride in his eyes.

"Yup. I've only skipped two, though, so I hear I'm headed for a record."

"I skipped five on my first go-around," Margaret said. "You're a brave woman."

At that moment, my phone rang in my pocket. I took it out and saw my mom's name on the caller ID.

"This is my parents. I should take it and wish them a Happy Thanksgiving."

Hayden squeezed my arm supportively, an innocent gesture without calling attention to the weight this call held. "Why don't you take it out on the terrace? It shouldn't be too miserable out there with the sun shining."

I nodded and crossed the room to the double doors leading to the balcony, hearing Preston say, "All right, it's sides time people," as I shut the door behind me.

"Hi, Mom. Happy Thanksgiving," I said, answering the call.

"Hi, Charlotte. Happy Thanksgiving. Your dad's here with me on speakerphone. Are you cooking at home today?"

"Oh, I'm with Hay—with my roommate's family at his brother's place today," I winced, referring to Hayden as my roommate, but I wasn't ready to open that box with my parents.

"That's nice he has family in the city. We're at the store. We'll be heading to Joe's Café to pick up to-go dinners on our way home soon."

"Oh, you're not cooking this year?" I asked, not able to keep the surprise out of my voice.

There was a pause. "No," my dad answered. "A lot of things are different this year."

"Don't tell me you're doing away with the bargain blind-date-with-a-book bin. The tourists will riot," I joked.

My parents laughed thinly. "No, the bin is ready to go," my dad answered.

"Is everything okay?" I asked, suddenly nervous by their tones.

"Well," my mom said. "We would have preferred to do this in person if you had been able to come home."

"Yeah, about that, I'm really sorry—"

"No, no," my mom interrupted. "Sorry, that wasn't supposed to make you feel guilty. Let's see, where should we start?"

"Your mom and I have been going to couple's counseling these last few months," my dad interjected.

"You have?" I said, very unsure where this was going.

"We have," my mom confirmed, sounding tired. "And I think what your dad is getting at is that the message would have always been the same, but the delivery has changed."

"Guys, I'm so confused. What's going on?"

My mom let out a big breath of air. "We're going to be closing the store. I'm not entirely sure when. It won't be until after the first of the year, but we're going to liquidate Ridge Reads."

I stood in stunned silence, not sure what to say.

"I had a bit of a breakthrough at our counseling session after my last conversation with you, and I realized I had been pretty unfair to you... about a lot of things, but especially about this internship. Just because your dreams are different from my dreams—our dreams—doesn't mean they're wrong."

"So, you're closing the store because I might not come back to take it over?" I asked, my fingers curling over the phone, like the tighter my grip on this piece of metal, the tighter my grip on my changing reality would remain.

"No," my dad said, sounding just as tired as my mom. "We're closing the store because we have to. Maybe if we hadn't resisted change, if we had invested in new technology or systems like you had suggested, things would be different."

"What the breakthrough helped us, well me, realize," my mom continued, "was while it would be an end of an era for our family, it would also free you up to do more, be more, than a family-run store in a small town."

"But what about a buyer? What about it becoming another family's dream?"

"We've put out some feelers. There are no bites. And we just don't have the capital to keep it afloat in the interim."

I paused. "The Bookstore Future Fund, they could—"

"You know as well as we do that you can only apply to the fund once every five years, Charlotte," Mom said gently.

"This isn't what I wanted"—a sob sounded in my throat—"I need you to know that."

"We do," my mom said. "And we're sorry to tell you on a day with your... friend's family, but we wanted to be sure you knew when you headed into that conversation about what your future with the IBA looked like."

"Thank you," I said, wiping my eyes. "I should probably get back soon. You guys enjoy dinner from Joe's and I'll talk to you soon, okay?"

"Sounds good. We love you, Charlotte," my dad said.

"And we'll expect you for the opening shift on December 16th. We have one more holiday season left in us," my mom said, sounding much more like her hardass self than the post-therapy woman I had been talking to for the past ten minutes.

I laughed a watery laugh. "I'm looking forward to it. Hopefully, I haven't forgotten how to run the register."

We hung up after that and I leaned on the railing, trying to process everything they had just told me.

I heard the door behind me open, feeling Hayden's presence with me on the balcony.

"Dinner's almost ready, and I thought you might want your coat. You've been out here a while," he said, draping my coat over my shoulders. I looked over at him, and his eyes widened, taking in what I assumed were red-rimmed eyes and wet cheeks. "Oh, babe, what's wrong? Are they mad you're not there?"

"My parents are in therapy," I started, laughing a little at how different the conversation we had was from other conversations during my adult life. "But, in more groundbreaking news, they're closing the store."

"Oh, baby, I'm so sorry," Hayden said, gathering me into his arms, causing tears to drip down my face anew. "Did they say why?"

"What I was always afraid of. They just can't keep up without upgrading their technology, and now it's too late."

"How did they seem?" he asked, his arm rubbing circles on my back.

"Did they blame me for leaving and therefore causing them to close? No, which, if not for the therapy, I would have expected them to. I'm still sort of waiting for that to happen. They were supportive of me pursuing where I could take my career with the Independent Bookstore Alliance. It was... a little surreal."

"So, how are you?" he said, stacking his chin on top of my head.

"I'm a little in shock. You know, I'm not really sure what I thought would happen to the store. I knew I didn't want to run it right now, but selfishly, I always wanted it to be there. To know I could fall back on it."

"You're not going to have to fall back on anything. Your star is just beginning to rise," Hayden said with deep sincerity, making me pull back and meet his eyes.

I rose a hand to cup his cheek. "Thank you," I said, infusing the words with as much feeling and gratefulness as I could muster.

The door opened again. Hunter stuck his head out. "Yo, love-birds, we're ready to eat."

Hayden huffed out an annoyed breath and turned to admonish his twin, but I put pressure on his arm to stop him. "It's okay," I said to him softly. Louder, I said, "I'm starving, let's eat." I wiped my fingers under my eyes and over my cheeks, hoping to hide any evidence of the tears. It would take some time to sort through all my feelings surrounding the idea that Ridge Reads wouldn't exist anymore, but those feelings would keep. It was time to eat Thanksgiving dinner with my boyfriend —definitely my boyfriend—and his family.

CHAPTER
Twenty~Four

HAYDEN

We all gathered around the table in Preston's club room. Dad and Preston argued over who should carve the turkey, before Dad caved and did the honors, to applause from everyone. It was strange, this space belonged to no one, and would be turned over to another user within the day, but it had been a long time since I felt so at home. A lot of that had to do with the woman sitting next to me.

Charlotte laughed at a story Spencer was telling her, picking up her wineglass and taking a sip. Spencer seemed to have let go of his final three questions, perhaps sensing the call with her parents hadn't gone particularly well. Charlotte was doing a great job of putting on a brave face and following the conversations taking place around the table, smiling and laughing in the right places, but not actively participating the way I knew she normally would.

Margaret clinked her wineglass to get our attention as everyone's eating wound down. "All right, boys, and Charlotte, please humor me for another year and go around the table saying what you're all thankful for. Preston, as our host, would you like to start?"

I snuck a glance at Charlotte, realizing I had forgotten to warn her about Margaret's tradition. Her attention was rapt on Margaret, not put off by the moment.

Preston picked up his drink. "I'm grateful that in a little over a month, it will officially be an election year, and we'll be out of the planning stages and into the action."

We all raised our glasses in a toast and took a sip, a Brandt twist on Margaret's tradition we had started once everyone was twenty-one.

Margaret, seated to Preston's right, went next. "I'm grateful for another year with my Brandt boys, and for expanding our circle to include new faces as well." Margaret's answer was the same every year, which was ironic considering it was her game, but it made my dad tear up every time.

"I'm grateful Hayden is back in the same city as one, sometimes two, of his brothers," Dad said, taking his turn. "We were worried about you in Boston by yourself. It's good to be around family."

I felt my cheeks burn slightly. Charlotte squeezed my knee in acknowledgment of my emotional overload as we all took another sip.

"I'm grateful for only having another year and a half left of this post doc," Spencer answered. "I'm ready to move forward with what's next."

It was my turn next. Maybe it was Dad's show of emotion that gave me strength, but I decided to go for it.

"I'm grateful for my family, mostly Duncan, for hiring horrible assistants, so when my life flipped upside down, my crash landing was softened by the beautiful woman sitting next to me. And I guess I'm grateful Charlotte's pranks didn't carry an overly vindictive streak, and that she gave me another chance."

Charlotte's eyes met mine, hers glistening with unshed tears. She cleared her throat, realizing it was her turn to go.

"Well, first, if it's okay, I'd like to say the book I'm most grateful for that I read this year. That's a little Reid family

Thanksgiving tradition my parents and I always liked to share. The book I'm most grateful for is *Don't Look, Just Leap*. I don't always read memoirs, but this one really gave me the courage to shake things up in my life and brought me to DC, where I got to share this day with all of you. So, I guess what I'm most grateful for is new beginnings."

I lifted Charlotte's hand off my leg and placed a kiss on the back of her hand.

Hunter shifted in his seat on the other side of Charlotte.

"Well damn, I have to follow these two?"

Everyone laughed quietly.

"Charlotte, everyone here will tell you my usual answers are the least emotional of anyone's. I think I was grateful for my motorcycle for at least three years in a row. But I'm going to switch it up this year and say I'm grateful you've entered our orbit. I've never seen adult Hayden as scared as he was when he thought he fucked things up with that llama prank, or as happy as he is today."

I looked over Charlotte's head to meet Hunter's eyes. I saw discontent flash across his face so fast anyone who didn't share a twin thing with him would have missed it. I nodded my head, letting him know I had him, whatever he needed, and he nodded back.

"Well," Margaret said, wiping her eyes. "We've come a long way from our first Thanksgiving together a decade and a half ago. I think Spencer was thirteen and thankful he had just gotten his braces off and could try my caramel squares. Who's ready for pie?"

We all murmured our general agreement, and Margaret, Dad, and Preston went off to get dessert prepped and ready.

"Hey," I said to Charlotte in a low voice, causing her to turn and look at me.

"Hi," she said back.

"Good Thanksgiving?" I asked, recognizing it was a loaded question.

"It's ending on a high note," she said with a small smile, titling her face up so I could lay a peck on her lips.

"Okay, gross," Spencer said from my other side. "Question seventeen. Charlotte, if you could have any superpower, what would it be?"

"Mine would be the ability to crush annoying little brothers," I said casually, pulling away from Charlotte, but leaving my arm slung across the back of her chair.

"Not a superpower, and I didn't ask you."

"Well, I'm not sure mine is a superpower either, but I'd like to have the ability to super-speed read. There are too many books in the world and not enough time."

"Nerd," Spencer coughed into his fist.

"Says the post-doc." Charlotte took his teasing in stride.

Spencer toasted her with his glass. "Point well taken, ma'am."

The dessert brigade returned with sliced pies, ice cream, and small plates, but quickly realized there was nowhere to put them, as we had never cleared the table. After a few moments of hubbub, we decided to serve our own desserts from the island and retire to the couches and chairs around the TV and electric fireplace, leaving the table as a problem for later us.

"So, Charlotte, forgive the follow-up on your grateful toast, but I got the feeling you weren't only referring to a new beginning with our boy Hayden here," Margaret said, breaking a comfortable silence.

"Oh," Charlotte said. "Well, you're right. I have a big meeting with my boss at the IBA the week after next to wrap up my internship and see if there's a permanent place for me. So, I'll know more soon."

"Well, that's very exciting! But I have to ask. Your mother didn't seem too thrilled with your internship in our conversation that set up you staying in Duncan's place. What does you staying on with IBA mean for Ridge Reads?"

Charlotte put her fork down.

"Well, it seems my parents are going to close the store sometime early next year, whether I stay at the IBA or not." Her voice shook a little. "Sorry, that's only the second time I've said that out loud. It's still a little surreal. They told me when we talked earlier. I apologize if I was a little quiet at dinner."

"It's hard to get a word in edge-wise with these four around," Dad said. "I have three decades of experience to show for that."

Charlotte laughed softly, acknowledging my dad's attempt at defusing some of the sadness.

"They're just going to close the store? Not try to sell it?" Margaret pressed. She had this way of interrogating you that felt slightly invasive and yet therapeutic all at once. I wondered if I should intervene, but met Margaret's eyes, and she made a gesture with her hand, indicating she had a plan and I should trust her.

Charlotte shook her head. "Apparently there isn't a ton of interest, and part of me wonders if my mom just can't stand the idea of seeing the store owned by someone else who might change the name or the focus from her family's store."

"Hmm, I wonder—"

"Margaret Hayes, you are not buying that store."

Margaret laughed. "No, of course not, dear. I mean, I love the store and want it to stay in our town, but that would tie us down too much from our travels and retirement. I was just wondering if there was something the Independent Book Alliance could do in a situation like this."

Charlotte shook her head. "There is a fund stores can apply to when they get in trouble. The gala for that fund was one of my main projects during my internship, but there's a limit on how often a store can benefit. We had to access the fund to stay open during the pandemic, so we wouldn't be eligible again."

Margaret nodded, the shrewd businesswoman she was in her past life coming through. "That makes sense. What about another branch of similar resources? Where the community wants to keep the store in it, but doesn't have the ability to fund the operations. The IBA could come in and provide oversight, and yes, some funds, until the store is solvent and then can be cooperatively owned by the town or community itself?"

Charlotte looked at Margaret intensely, her brow furrowed as it did when she was thinking hard about something.

"That's really interesting, Margaret. Can we get coffee at some point before you and Stephen go back to Holly Ridge? I'd love to talk more about this when my brain isn't so full of wine and turkey, and it's had some time to process."

Margaret looked pleased that Charlotte had asked. "I would love that, dear. We'll make it happen."

Then she turned her powers on me. "And what about you, Hayden? Are you enjoying your CIO position?"

I looked at Charlotte, wondering how honest I should be, given the reminders I'd had just this evening of the gossips that my brothers were.

"The more I've climbed up the ladder at Brandt Investing International, the less I've actually gotten to work with people and computers, so I've been struggling with that. And, uh, I don't actually know that I like living in a big city?"

"But you've lived in one city or another since college," Hunter pointed out, like I was an idiot who didn't realize that.

"Yeah, I know, but they've always seemed cold? And impersonal? But, since we're analyzing people's grateful messages, as Dad pointed out, I haven't lived in a big city with a brother, or with someone... special." I snuck a glance at Charlotte. "Perhaps I don't have to change everything all at once."

Margaret beamed at me, pleased that I was soul-searching.

"But none of you can say anything to Duncan about this, okay? I mean it. He's back in the States for that week at the beginning of December and I'm going to talk to him then. I have... ideas."

Preston snorted. I gave him my best stink eye. "I mean it, *Gossip Girl*. Not a word to Duncan. Or you know... Alamo."

Preston looked at me with panic in his eyes, nodding. "Not a word. Got it."

My dad muttered, scraping up the last of the whipped cream from his plate. "One of these days, you all are going to realize you're grown-ass adults and tell me what these one-word threats mean. The suspense is torture."

We all laughed and Hunter picked up the remote to turn the TV back on for the evening football game, sensing the soul-searching conversation was over.

"No, no. We're on dish duty." My dad indicated to me, Spencer and Hunter, heaving himself out of his chair. "It's the least we can do after these three worked so hard to cook this meal for us."

"But I put the butter on the butter dish," Spencer whined, uncurling himself from the recliner he was lounging in all the same.

"How the hell do you feed yourself on a regular basis if that's your idea of cooking," Hunter said, giving him a little shove toward the kitchen, causing Spencer to shove him back.

After getting up to join in on the cleanup, I placed a kiss on Charlotte's hairline. "Don't move. I'll be back before you know it."

Charlotte smiled up at me. "I'm not going anywhere."

Twenty~Five

CHARLOTTE

Thanksgiving had never been what I considered a ground-breaking holiday. Honestly, if I thought about it too long, it was sort of gross, given what happened between the settlers and Native Americans outside of that one day. But what I found this year at that Brandt family meal—for myself, and for Hayden and me—was something I couldn't ignore.

My parents and I talked a few times after Thanksgiving. I didn't want to get their hopes up, as I had no idea Paula would go for our community-run store idea or how the timing would line up. I just encouraged them to keep news of the sale quiet, given the holiday shopping season. They asked questions about my internship each time we spoke, but never mentioned what would happen next. Things were progressing, but change doesn't happen overnight.

When we weren't at our day jobs, Hayden and I could be found side by side, working on our different proposals. Whether we were on the couch or sitting at the kitchen island, there was a feeling of rightness each time I looked up from my laptop screen to find Hayden looking at me, a content smile on his face. We found we needed to set benchmarks we had to reach each night before we could enjoy each other physically, though I'd be lying if I didn't admit those benchmarks felt fairly fluid some of those nights. The promise of orgasms and time spent laying in Hayden's arms were quite the motivator, it turned out. I felt more prepared for my meeting with Paula than ever before.

I shut my laptop with a satisfying click, leaning back into the couch cushions and looked over at Hayden's handsome face, washed in the blue light from his screen. His brow was furrowed, his lips moving as he read over his words. Delivery from District Taco was on its way. We made a deal we would work until dinner arrived, and then we'd spend the rest of the evening relaxing. Duncan was currently in DC for a few days before he had to return to Europe for the rest of the year, so Hayden's meeting lined up with mine. This was probably for the best for our mutual focus benefits.

"I can feel you looking at me, Char. I have"—Hayden peaked at this phone—"ten more minutes until the food gets here."

"I know, I know. Just enjoying the view a bit, okay? Is that a crime?"

He looked over at me with an indulgent smile. "I like looking at you too, babe. I plan to look at *all* of you, just after I crush a burrito bowl."

"Mmm, post-bean sexy times. Very appealing."

He waggled his eyebrows. "I left the beans off this time. You're in for a treat. Now, give me my nine more minutes, please."

I giggled, picking up my phone, granting his request. I had texts from Austin and Blaire wishing me luck at my meeting tomorrow, which I answered, promising them each a phone call as soon as I knew something.

I thumbed through social media, which at this point was mostly a mixture of people from high school interspersed with accounts for independent bookstores across the country. I looked at all the events and specials different stores were hosting in December, tucking away anything extra special that stood out.

Hayden's phone vibrated. "That's the delivery driver. They just buzzed into the building. Food will be up in a minute."

"I'll grab plates and drinks. Beer for you?"

"Yes, please."

I walked into the kitchen, grabbing what we would need for dinner. Hayden stood from the couch and stretched, groaning, his shirt riding up to reveal a sliver of toned abs above his waistband.

"Keep on table setting over there, missy," Hayden teased, catching me ogling him. "Dinner first. I believe you made that rule, Miss Hangry Pants."

"Stupid rule," I muttered, returning to the fridge to grab a beer for each of us just as there was a knock on the door.

Hayden met the delivery person and brought the bag into the space, wafting delicious scents of our Mexican food feast. I heard my stomach growl.

"Mmhm, see," Hayden said, doling out my tacos and his bowl onto the plates I laid out, setting a bag of chips between us to share.

"Okay, fine, your wisdom prevails again," I said, rolling my eyes as I unwrapped the foil from my first taco.

We ate in silence for a few minutes, the crinkle of paper and crunch of chips accompanying the ambient sounds of the city fifteen stories below us as background noise.

"So, tomorrow. Big day, huh?" Hayden said, scooping more of his burrito bowl onto his fork.

"Just potentially life changing for both of us. No big deal," I joked, the dryness of my tone revealing my true nerves.

"So, uh, yeah, for both of us. As individuals and a collective us, right?" Hayden said.

"Yes, that's true," I said casually, like I hadn't thought of this exact topic in quiet moments over the past week.

"You're pitching a lot of ideas to Paula tomorrow. Is there one you want more than others?"

"Well, I think my heart and soul is invested in this community-owned bookstore idea. But there's always the chance Paula thinks it's a great idea and wants to make it happen, but won't let me work on it, given my personal investment in Ridge Reads."

"Hmm," Hayden hummed affirmatively.

"Of the open positions Paula gave me to look at, I think I'm most interested in either the fundraising role, which would keep me here in DC or the membership engagement associate job. That job would have me traveling around visiting our different member stores across the country, seeing what they need from us or how we can help them given our existing services they may not be taking advantage of. With that job, I'm not sure where I would be based. Maybe back in Holly Ridge at my parents' house since I'd be traveling so much. Save on rent."

I bit my lip as I snuck a peek at Hayden's face, which gave nothing away.

"Well, they're definitely going to offer you something. I think Paula giving you that list of positions all but confirms that."

I nodded. "I hate feeling this confident, because I feel like I'm going to jinx something, but I think you're right. My nerves are more related to the uncertainty of what's next."

Hayden let out a breath.

"I feel that. I can't decide if Duncan is going to scream at me for wasting his time and not want to hear another word from me or just rip apart my proposal as a dumb idea when he hears it."

"Or he could love it and have input on how to make it better, Mr. Negative."

"Yeah, I guess." Hayden looked like a lost little boy and I'd never seen him this way before.

I spun in my seat so I was fully facing Hayden.

"I know I don't know Duncan, considering he's been galli-vanting around Europe the whole time we've known each other, but from what you've told me, he loves you and wants what's best for you."

"Yeah, as long as it doesn't mess with his bottom line."

"I have a hard time believing that even his money would

stand in the way of wanting you to be happy. Support and love seems to be what the Brandt family is built on."

"I know you're right. It's just hard to remember we're both functional adults when sometimes I still feel like I'm thirteen, watching my big brother work hard to keep our family together when he was just a kid himself. I just want to make him proud."

I put my hand on Hayden's arm. "You will. By going after what you want and not what you think everyone else wants. He'll know he helped raise you right."

Hayden tangled his fingers in mine.

"So," I said slowly, afraid of the answer. "What did all that market research tell you was the best place for you to start your business?"

"Well, there's Atlanta, Nashville, Palo Alto, and then, Washington DC. Assuming you're right, I'm hoping Duncan might have some suggestions and connections."

"All big cities. All over the country... huh," I said, my eyes focused on where our hands joined.

"It does seem that way, but cities have suburbs. I'm hoping I could find a happy medium." His voice sounded uncertain as his thumb rubbed the back of my hand.

"So. Sounds like it might be a bigger day for each of us rather than the collective us tomorrow," I said, after a strained silence.

"I would really like it to be a big day for the collective us," Hayden said, his tone laced with meaning.

I looked up, meeting his eyes, so full of emotion. Fear, hope, uncertainty, affection.

"There you go, thinking about what others might want of you instead of what's best for you."

Hayden swallowed. "What if you're what's best for me?"

My breath hitched, tears springing to my eyes. This beautiful man offered so much and part of me wanted to take it, to be selfish and ask him to factor me into whatever he did next. But I couldn't do that just when he was finding himself in the world.

"Come here," I said, bringing my mouth to his, losing myself in a slow and gentle kiss full of so much longing and promise. Slow and sensual, our mouths moved together, Hayden pulling me until I was sitting in his lap, straddling him with my back to the island, the remains of our dinner forgotten.

"You have an especially early start tomorrow," I said, brushing his hair back off his forehead. "How about a bath and an early night in bed?"

"Do we have to sleep in bed?" Hayden asked, a wicked gleam in his eye, his earlier question seemingly forgotten.

"Why do you think I'm suggesting bed at 7:00 p.m.?" I said suggestively, grinding my hips into his lap.

With coordination I'd never understand, Hayden pushed out his chair, forcing me to wrap my legs around him like a koala to feel secure.

"Early bird catches the worm, after all," he said, walking us toward his room. An evening where it was just the two of us, blocking out the outside world and what tomorrow would bring, was exactly what we needed.

Twenty-Six

HAYDEN

The car carried me toward the office while it was still dark out. Since Duncan was only in the States for a few days, he was trying to stay mostly on European time. This meant people he could inconvenience, like his brother, were scheduled to meet with him at the balls-ass early time of 5:30 a.m.

Normally, leaving a warm bed with an enticing woman in it would have made a cold winter's morning like this one even more miserable. This morning though, I had been awake since about three, listening to Charlotte breathe and thinking about what the day would bring. She was probably right to cut off our conversation about what today's meetings could mean for us as a couple, but that didn't stop my mind from spinning through possibilities. I slid silently from the bed before my alarm, dressing in the dark, and leaving her with a kiss on the head. I left a good luck note and the coffee maker all set up for her when she woke, but this morning felt like something I had to face on my own, the knowledge she'd be rooting for me enough.

I took the elevator to the fifth floor, where Duncan's office was. I rounded the corner to his suite, slightly shocked to see a yawning Bradley in his seat at assistant's desk at this early hour. I gave him a sympathetic smile, wondering if this particular assistant would quit before he gave Duncan a reason to fire him, forcing him to keep the same hours without the benefit of the weeks abroad. He'd made it this far, maybe this one would stick.

"Hay—I mean, Mr. Brandt. Good morning. Mr. Brandt is expecting you. Will you be needing any coffee or anything this morning?"

I lifted my travel cup in answer. "I'm all set, thank you, Bradley"

"Go on in," he answered, looking relieved at not having to find the energy to make me a cup of coffee. It was likely Duncan was on his second or third cup already.

I knocked on the door as I entered and found Duncan's head bent over some spreadsheets. He waved me in, intent on finishing the page he was on before looking up. I walked in and took a seat at one of the chairs across from his desk. Taking a few minutes to look around his office, I noted there were a lot of things in the office that screamed "Duncan Brandt, CEO and powerful millionaire," but very few that screamed "Duncan Brandt, big brother and normal human." You would never be able to tell he ran half-marathons, loved volunteering at animal shelters, or collected bottles of whisky from the cold and impersonal office he kept.

Duncan put his pen down and finally looked up from his desk, surprised to find me sitting down across from him. He got up from his chair and rounded his desk.

"What, you don't see me for six months, after living in my condo for most of that, and you can't even wait to give your big brother a hug?"

I stood up, accepting a tight squeeze and the firm back slaps he offered.

"It's good to see you, Dunc."

"You too, Hayden. So, tell me, what's up? I know it's not work-related. We have the executive cabinet meeting all day tomorrow."

I swallowed. "Well, it is sort of work-related. I think I need to resign as your Chief Information Officer."

Duncan's eyes widened slightly. It was the only outward sign I had caught him off guard.

"I see. Is there something wrong with your team? The distribution of duties? Your salary?"

"Oh, fuck off, you know you pay me entirely too much for my first executive-level job. It's not the salary."

"So, the team then—"

"It's nothing to do with the team, the company, anything like that. It's me."

Duncan leaned back in his chair, crossing his arms. "Okay, then, tell me more."

I took in a big breath. Here went nothing.

"Well, first off, I hate living in a big city. The past few months have been decent, but it's just so much all the time. The higher I climbed with the company after grad school, the less I got to poke around computers and figure things out."

Duncan nodded, showing me he was listening, bolstering me with the strength to keep going.

"Moving up meant I got to work directly with people using the systems less. Work became all about meetings and reports, and making decisions that cascaded in ways I couldn't completely understand because I wasn't working with the systems or with the people, just making choices that impacted them."

"I see. So, what would you do instead?"

I examined Duncan's face, but he wasn't giving anything away. I took a few more deep breaths and plowed forward.

"I want to consult on technology for small businesses. Do audits of their systems and processes, suggest improvements and new software or hardware they could benefit from, if appropriate. If not, then I'd put them in touch with someone who could help with their niche. I want to help businesses thrive, not just survive, and level up to reach their next benchmark or goal.

Maybe through that I'll find a common need across industries and be able to develop software or an app that can help. But I just want to be out there with the people, not in a corner office avoiding them."

Duncan was quiet for a moment, before he leaned forward, putting his elbows on his knees and looking at me intensely.

"You really hate living in cities?"

"That's what you took away from all that?"

"Okay, let me rephrase. Do you really hate living in cities, or do you just hate feeling alone?"

That gave me pause as I thought it over. Duncan continued.

"You know, I've always been good with being alone. That's why as much travel as I do works for me. But for you, well, first off, you're a twin, so you weren't even alone in the womb. I was surprised when you went off to Boston for college, but I was excited for you. I thought Hunter might follow you and break away... well, we both know Hunter only follows his own path. But, in any case, why do you think this fall hasn't been so bad?"

"Because I've only been here for a few months, so I don't know it well enough to hate it yet?"

Duncan shook his head.

"Okay, oh wise one. Go ahead and Yoda me. I can tell you want to."

"Well, for one thing, Preston is here. Didn't you see him each week?"

"I mean, yeah, we got dinner a lot..."

"And what about your girl?"

"Charlotte? I mean, she's just a roommate." I wasn't sure why I lied in that moment, but I felt exposed enough as it was.

"Oh, now *you* fuck off with that. Preston may not have told me about your discontent with your job when I asked him what this meeting was about, the little gossipy traitor, but he did blab all about you and Charlotte at Thanksgiving. Said he'd never seen you look at a woman that way, not that we've met any of your girls in the past few years."

"Okay, yes, fine. I'm not sure why I said she was just my roommate—"

"Because you're in love with her, and to admit that to me is to have to admit it to yourself?"

"I'm not in love with... am I in love with Charlotte?"

"Hayden," Duncan said gently, the way you do with a child when they're being a real idiot. "You donated twenty thousand dollars of the company's money, so she would stay home with you and get better."

I looked at my big brother, my boss.

"I think I may have fallen in love with her when she sat with me on the couch and asked me inane questions about *Star Wars*."

Duncan looked triumphant at his breakthrough.

"But what does that have to do with me no longer being your CIO?"

"Well, I wanted to confirm that you *could* be happy living in a city, as long as you had the right people around you."

"Okay..."

"What if you opened up your consulting business as part of Brandt Investing International? I've been toying with the idea of a small business arm for a while. So much of our work is with these big companies, but not with smaller companies for whom a fraction of our normal funding could make a world of difference. I think your vision could be a part of that. Why wouldn't they want to work with us, if we could offer them funding *and* technological expertise? It would set us apart."

"You would do that for me?"

"I'm not doing anything *for* you, Hayden. You've earned this. I'm sure that folder you're clutching there has a bunch of projections and research that backs that up. I'd let you walk out that door if I thought that's what was best and would make you truly happy, but this way we get to keep working together, you get to be in the same city as Preston and sometimes me, and you get to keep your girl."

The smile that had been growing on my face fell off when Duncan mentioned keeping Charlotte.

"What's that face? You don't get to keep the girl? Did you do something stupid?"

"Ha. I don't think so. I'm just not sure I'll get to keep her. Charlotte has a very similar type of meeting with her boss this morning and not all outcomes of that end with her staying in DC."

Duncan nodded.

"Well then, you'll run this new venture from wherever she is, maybe. I bet we can make it work as long as it's on the East Coast."

I sat back in my chair, a little stunned.

"Let's keep talking about it. I assume you were going to give me a long notice, anyway?"

"Oh yes, of course. I figured at least three months."

Duncan nodded.

"Okay, perfect. Let's plan on you staying CIO through the first quarter of next year, and we'll keep talking about how we can make a place for your new venture within Brandt Investing International. Now, get the hell out of my office and go get some real work done. I need to give my assistant something to do besides sleep out there."

I laughed and stood up, suddenly much less depressed about going up to my office than I had been in the last few weeks.

"Thanks, Duncan. I'll see you tomorrow for that meeting, if not before." I extended my hand to shake his.

Duncan had the same firm handshake he had when he was helping me practice for my first college interview during my junior year of high school.

He rounded the side of his desk, returning to his CEO chair, as I turned to make my way out of his office.

"Oh, and Hayden, I'm going to be in DC a lot more starting in January. I'm making some hires in the UK and in Germany that should mean less travel for me. I hope that will add to the things that make DC a city you would want to live in."

I turned back to see Duncan was facing away from me, looking out the window. Perhaps he wasn't quite as good at being alone as he thought.

"It definitely will, Dunc."

He turned around and smiled at me.

"Now, I'm going to go scare the shit out of your assistant, I'm assuming he's nodded off by now. Take it easy on him, okay?"

"I make no such promises."

Twenty-Seven

CHARLOTTE

"Come on in, Charlotte," Paula waved me in, throwing away the remnants of her lunch in the trash can under her desk. "I don't make a habit of eating at my desk, but we're taking a two-week Alaskan cruise this year for Christmas, so I'm trying to fit a month's worth of year-end tasks into two weeks."

"Noted," I smiled. "I do very much appreciate the commitment the IBA has to work-life balance."

Paula smiled back. "I know you mean that sincerely or else I'd tell you to stop sucking up. You already have a permanent place here if you want one. We just need to figure out what."

I felt some of the tension go out of my spine. Now I could enjoy most of this conversation, even pitching my heart and soul in project form.

"So, before we get into the specifics, I've been really excited to hear about any ideas or initiatives you've been dreaming up during your months with us."

"Well, I do have something. It's probably a bit bigger than what you may have had in mind for me to bring to this meeting, but..." I trailed off.

"Everything has to start somewhere. I can't wait. Please, dive right in," Paula smiled encouragingly.

I looked down at my notes, but knew I could do this by heart, so I looked up and met Paula's eyes instead.

"As you know, my parents own a bookstore. Ridge Reads."

Paula nodded.

"Well, unfortunately, it looks like the store isn't going to survive. Getting into the why and how isn't important. Talking with my parents, and my boyfriend's stepmother, who's a big supporter of our store, made me realize that there may be an opportunity for the IBA to help stores beyond the Bookstore Future Fund. My parents received money from the fund within the last five years, so they're not eligible again. But what if the IBA was able to step in with funding and support a transition to a community co-op owned business? Of course, there would have to be parameters—a maximum amount of debt, a minimum number of years in business, interest and availability from members of the community—but I think this could work. I think this could help keep bookstores in communities that really need them and love them when circumstances just don't allow for stores to stay open under traditional means."

I handed Paula a copy of my proposal and my research and she flipped through it for a few brief moments.

"This is a great idea, Charlotte. It's a leap forward for the Bookstore Future Fund and the IBA in general. And I love the idea of creating a community co-op board for a handoff after a certain timeline. We wouldn't want it to seem like the Independent Bookstore Alliance was getting into the business of creating a block of stores."

I nodded. "Indie bookstores are all about serving the community they're in, so I figured why not use that focus to ensure stores can continue to serve their communities for years to come?"

Paula tapped her pen on her desk.

"This will take a significant increase in the Bookstore Future

Fund, if not the creation of an offshoot fund all together. But there is a grant we were awarded that the use for hasn't been decided yet. Do you think your parents would be open to something like this?"

I felt my heart rate increase.

"I haven't mentioned it to them at all. I didn't want them to get their hopes up. They are very much talking about closing and not finding a buyer, mostly because they have no leads on someone who would keep Ridge Reads what our family has built it to be. But this, being spearheaded by the community, I have to believe they would go for it."

Paula nodded, her face still pensive.

"And these projects? This is what you would want to work on?"

I paused for a moment before answering.

"You know, until you actually asked me that question in real time, I thought my answer would have been yes. But I think knowing Ridge Reads has a chance would be enough. I want to take the fundraising job. I would still be supporting this initiative, because, like you said, it's going to take a lot more funds than we've had before, but I would be helping more than just Ridge Reads, which is what I came to DC, to the IBA, to do."

Paula nodded, a proud smile crossing her face.

"I do think you'd be perfect for the fundraising role, because you'll be fueled by the passion of the potential for all the good the fund could do."

I nodded, a bit speechless.

"So, forgive a bit of personal probing, but you mentioned a boyfriend and his stepmother who knows Ridge Reads... is this a boyfriend back at home, who's going to hate us for taking you away from him?"

"Oh! No." I felt my cheeks turn red. "You remember my roommate, Hayden, the CIO from Brandt Investing International, who was at the gala? He and I are... together. Well,

I think so. I mean, we are, but I hope we still will be, now that I'm staying here?"

Paula looked pleased to hear this news.

"From what I saw at the gala, that handsome young man was a big Charlotte guy. I bet he'll be thrilled to hear you're staying. But if you met him here, how is his family connected to Ridge Reads?"

"Right! His stepmom and dad live in Holly Ridge now and she's a big supporter of the store. She'd actually be an excellent person for the co-op board, if things do move forward in that direction for the store."

"Oh, excellent. I was hoping you'd have some leads. Why don't you talk to your parents about these ideas and see if they'd be interested in being a test case for this new process? I'll have to get a few things going here before I leave for my trip, so keep their expectations as tempered as possible, but I have a good feeling."

The smile that crossed my face threatened to split my cheeks in two, but I couldn't help it.

"Thank you, Paula, I mean, for everything. For taking a chance on me, trusting me with the gala and something so new to me, for listening to me and my ideas now. I'm just so thrilled to be staying here and working with you."

Paula's typical warm smile returned to her face.

"It's going to be great new year. Now, why don't you plan on ending your internship at the end of the week as scheduled, so you can go home and help with the holiday season at your parents' store like you had planned? We'll get your paperwork to HR and put your first official day as the new Associate for Fundraising Initiatives as the first Monday after the start of the new year."

I nodded. "That sounds great. It's funny, I came here not being able to wait for a break from the store and now, I can't wait to get back and work some shifts."

"You know, that doesn't sound funny to me at all. It sounds

like someone who's rediscovered their love for the place that made them who they are today. Now, get out of my office. Someone's just given me a lot more work to do."

Paula softened this with a smile, and I got up, trying to keep myself from bouncing all the way down the hall to my cubicle.

I took my phone out of my desk drawer, pulling up my text thread with Hayden.

HAYDEN (8:24 AM)

I hope your coffee was extra delicious this morning. Can't wait to see you tonight.

(Charlotte loved this message at 9:17 AM)

CHARLOTTE (3:46 PM)

I have some great news. I can't wait to tell you. See you at home.

I sat back down at my desk, clicking into our project management software, refreshing myself with the fundraisers the fund had coming up soon. It was time to shake down some donors. The IBA had big goals and a new official employee to make them happen.

CHAPTER
Twenty-Eight

HAYDEN

I reached the condo door, finding it already unlocked, and followed the sound of music to Charlotte's room. I hadn't answered her text from this afternoon, leaving the office as soon as I could to find out what "great news" meant in this case.

I pushed open the door to find Charlotte dancing around the room, a cardboard box in the middle of her bed, as she put the many books she had collected over the past several months in it. I felt my stomach drop. *Why was she packing?*

"Knock, knock," I said, my knuckles knocking on the door at the same time. *Smooth, Brandt, real smooth.*

"Hey babe, you're home!" Charlotte exclaimed, rushing over toward me to give me a kiss on the cheek before returning to her box.

"So, how did it go today?" I asked cautiously.

"It went so great. Paula absolutely loved the co-op community-owned idea. She's hoping we can use Ridge Reads as a test case."

"That's great news," I said, hoping the cheer in my voice didn't sound forced. "So, you're headed back to Holly Ridge to head that up?"

"Oh, no"—she stopped moving around the room and looked up at me—"didn't you get my text? I said I had great news."

"Right... and when you said she loved the idea that would save your parents' store..."

"Oh, duh. Sorry, I have so much adrenaline rushing through me, which is why I started packing, because I *hate* packing. She did ask me if I wanted to work on that project, but I realized I wanted the fundraising job more. So I'm staying here, in DC, and going to keep working with Paula. The fundraising arm will help raise funds for the co-op community store initiative, so I'll still be helping Ridge Reads, but this way, I'll be helping stores everywhere, which is what I came to DC and the IBA to do. So, you see, great news."

"Okay, yes. Great," I said, still confused. If she was staying, why was she packing? What did that mean?

Charlotte examined my face closely. "How did your meeting go? You seemed so positive this morning when you texted?"

"Oh, it went really well. Duncan was supportive of my idea, and actually wants me to do it through his company. There are some details to work out, but I'll be staying in DC too, it looks like."

"Hayden, that's amazing!" Charlotte bounded back over to me, smacking a kiss on my lips this time, pulling away before my brain could catch up.

"Let me just close up this box, and then we can fully debrief after we order dinner? Where is the tape? And the scissors. God, this is why I hate packing. I always lose things."

"Um, Charlotte?" I said, hating how shaky my voice sounded. Charlotte must have heard it too, because she abandoned her search and wheeled back around.

"What's wrong, Hayden? Oh no, you're upset you're staying in DC? Did Duncan make it seem like you can't say no?"

"No, no, nothing like that." I shook my head. "I just, um, don't understand why you're packing if you're staying in DC?"

"Oh, that. My agreement with Duncan to stay here is up on

Sunday, so like I said, just using the adrenaline to get a head start. I don't want to spend all weekend packing when we could be hanging out, especially because I'm headed back to Holly Ridge and you all are headed to meet Duncan in Paris for Christmas... Oh God, I guess I need to find somewhere to live, huh? Where are you going to look? It would be nice to not be on opposite sides of the city. I mean, if that's what you want, I'm sort of jumping ahead here. We really should order some dinner so we can talk. Where is that fucking tape?"

I felt my smile get bigger the longer Charlotte rambled. She wasn't trying to get away from me. She just didn't have all the information yet. God, she was cute.

I took out my phone and typed something quickly, hitting send.

"So, I guess that means you didn't get my text?" mirroring her words from earlier as I put my phone back in my pocket.

"Oh shoot, you texted? I guess my phone is hiding with the tape..."

"They're both on the dresser there," I said, pointing.

Charlotte cheered, grabbing her phone with one hand and the roll of tape with the other. I saw her swipe on my text. She read it, looked up at me, and then back at the phone, likely to be sure she read it right.

HAYDEN (6:06 PM)

Stay here and live with me?

I walked toward her. "Duncan's decided to look for a new place when he comes back to the city next year, something closer to the office, because the guy needs a reason to be more of a workaholic."

"So, we could live here. Together."

I nodded. "Something about not wanting to live in his little brother's sex den. I dunno. I tuned out when I heard him say the words 'sex den.'" I shuddered as I remembered those words coming out of Duncan's mouth.

"So, I don't have to pack? I don't have to move? And we get to stay together... in DC?"

I nodded. "Though I would request you move things officially into the master. It does have the better shower, you know."

Charlotte's eyes filled with unshed tears, throwing her arms around my neck and burying her head in my chest.

"I mean, you can keep using the other shower if it means that much to you," I joked, wrapping my arms around her and breathing her in.

Charlotte laughed wetly, and she smacked my chest. "It's just been an overwhelming day, okay? I mean, I left here this morning not sure we would live in the same city in a month, and now you're saying I get to see you every day *and* I don't have to move, after I secured my dream job? It's a lot for a girl to take in, ya know."

I laughed, leaning down to give her a peck. "I do know."

She looked up at me. "This is all wonderful, but I still need to be sure. This would mean you would live in DC, in the city, and be okay with it? You're not doing it for me or for Duncan? Or even for Preston? But you, Hayden Andrew Brandt, want it?"

"Fucking Hunter," I ground out, "giving you the power to middle name me."

She shrugged, waiting for my answer.

"I don't think it was the city living I had a problem with. I think it was the fact that I was one of millions and still felt so lonely. Having my brothers near helps that, but really, I owe so much of it to you. You make me feel like I'll never be lonely again."

Charlotte's eyes welled once more.

"And I know you said it's been an overwhelming day, but I hope you can take one more thing. I love you, Charlotte Emma Reid."

Charlotte's mouth broke into a huge grin.

"I love you too, Hayden Andrew Brandt. Now kiss me, in *our* condo, before I lose my mind."

I bent my head and did just that, only for Charlotte to pull away a moment later.

"Austin? Is that where you got the middle name from?"

I shrugged. "You don't have any siblings. He seemed like the next best thing."

Charlotte laughed and pulled my head back down to hers. All thoughts of packing, middle names, and even dinner, forgotten.

Epilogue

CHARLOTTE

I returned from Holly Ridge mid-afternoon on December 31st. Hayden's flight was getting into Dulles soon, but getting through customs and back to the city from outside the Beltway was going to take a while. I had offered to pick him up, but considering we'd both turn around and climb in another taxi, he insisted he meet me back at our place. *Our place.* That still didn't seem real. It was weird not being with Hayden the past few weeks, but it was good too—to be home, seeing my parents and a happily-engaged Blaire and a still-chronically-single Austin. It felt like I was leaving Holly Ridge on the right terms when I boarded my flight this time around. I knew I could go back anytime I wanted to.

It was for the best I had a little time before Hayden arrived. I wanted to put together a few surprises for him. The stuff I'd ordered from Whole Foods—champagne, charcuterie, and New Year's hats, crowns and noisemakers—had been waiting at the concierge desk. I put on some jazz music, which just felt right for New Year's Eve, and moved around the apartment, setting things up. I pulled the gifts I brought back with me out of my luggage and wrapped them, putting them under the artificial tree

Hayden had insisted we get before I left for Holly Ridge, even though neither of us would be here to see it on actual Christmas. "It's our condo's first Christmas," Hayden had argued, "we can't leave it naked without a Christmas tree."

I suppose someone had to be not naked in this condo. I certainly hoped Hayden and I wouldn't be clothed for too long after he walked in the front door.

Hayden texted he had touched down on the runway at Dulles, and I took that as my cue to get in the shower and wash the airport germs off my skin. I curled my hair and put on a black skater dress with a low scoop neck. I usually wore tights with this number, especially in the winter because the skirt was pretty short, but I knew exactly what I was trying to do in leaving them off. I considered leaving the underwear off too, but then decided if there was a fire and I had to evacuate, I wanted my ass to have *some* covering.

Before I knew it, Hayden had texted he was on his way up, and I gave up any pretense of keeping my cool. I waited by the front door and threw my arms around his neck as soon as the door was open the whole way, sending him stumbling sideways into his luggage and the door jam.

"Hi there, babe," he said, his voice betraying his laughter as he wrapped his free hand around my waist, the other holding onto a few gift bags.

"Hi," I said into his neck. "I missed you."

"I missed you too."

The lack of teasing about my overenthusiastic greeting let me know just how much he meant it.

I stepped back, running my hand down his arm to tangle my fingers with his, not quite ready to stop touching him yet, but ready to let him enter the apartment.

"So, how was your flight?" I asked, grabbing his suitcase with my other hand. "Also, how do you smell so Hayden-y after nine hours on a plane?"

Hayden set the bags on the island, and I followed his lead,

nestling the roller bag under the lip of the counter. We'd unpack later.

Hayden's cheeks were a bit pink. "I may have stashed a travel vial of my cologne in my carry-on so I could spritz before I came up here. I know you like the scent."

I laughed. "You old softy. I love that. C'mere."

I pulled him in by the hand I still held and his lips met mine, locking something back into place that had been missing since I last saw him. Our kisses were slow and searching, the kind you shared when you knew you had all night.

"So," I mumbled against Hayden's mouth a few moments later. "Any of those gifts for me?"

Hayden pulled away, laughing. "They might be. So, gifts first, even though you're giving me all sorts of temptation in that skirt?"

I shimmied my hips, swishing the short skirt back and forth.

"Maybe you can consider this your final present?" *God, how cliché were we?*

Hayden's eyes heated. I guess cliché worked for us.

"I can work with that. Can I at least put them under the tree first?" Hayden turned to face the tree, the white lights softly glowing against the sliding door of the balcony.

"Or maybe not. I'm not sure I want my low-maintenance wrapping job next to those masterpieces of packages."

I pushed him gently toward the living room.

"It's an occupational hazard. We offer gift wrapping at the store every year. I got to brush up on my skills this month."

"How is the store? Are your parents still all in on the co-op owned idea?"

"Store's great, parents are great, but we're getting side-tracked. Presents, *presents,* then catch up, okay?"

Hayden put his newly emptied hands up in surrender, "Okay, okay, far be it from me to complain about that."

I bounced over, sitting on the ottoman from the sectional and grabbing Hayden's first present from under the tree.

"Here, this one first."

Hayden set on the floor next to the tree, facing me an arm's length away. He felt the package and laughed.

"A book?! I never would have guessed."

I rolled my eyes. "Just open it."

He ripped the paper with a satisfying tear. His eyes opened wide.

"The Mark Hamill memoir? And it's signed? But this isn't out for another three weeks?"

I waggled my eyebrows. "Bookish girlfriend perks. Though if you ever tell Penguin Random House you got it this early, I'll have to kill you."

Hayden started leafing through the pages, muttering "deal" distractedly. I let him go for another few seconds before clearing my throat.

"Right, right," Hayden shook his head. "Presents, *presents,* catch up, and then reading. Hmm, I was going to do this one last... but I think I'll give it to you now."

Hayden pulled a small bag out of where it was nestled in the tissue paper of one of the larger bags and handed it to me.

I took it from his outstretched hand and raised an eyebrow.

"Hayden Andrew, this looks like it broke our predetermined price limit."

Hayden shrugged. "Guilty. I only have a CIO salary for so much longer, and I wanted to spoil you a bit."

I rolled my eyes since his salary would drop from outrageous to simply extravagant, but pulled a small box out of the bag all the same. Taking off the lid, I raised my hand to my lips in a gasp.

"Hayden, it's gorgeous."

Nestled on a cotton backing was a necklace. The wire charm was twisted into the shape of a book. It was simple, very much my style, but held so much meaning, not only in the design, but in the thoughtful man who gave it to me.

He looked at me with a burning intensity in his eyes.

"I commissioned a jewelry maker at the Christmas market near Duncan's rented apartment to make it for you. I figured if I got you something with diamonds or gems on it, you'd only wear it on special occasions, and I wanted to get you something you'd wear daily, so you'd have a piece of me close to your heart. Because my heart is yours, but I know your heart belongs to books, as well as to me. This way, they can be closer than ever."

I put the lid carefully back on the box and set it next to me on the ottoman.

Hayden pursed his lips in confusion. "You're not going to put it on?"

"Oh, I will. There are just some other things I want to take off first."

At that, I moved off the ottoman and joined Hayden on the floor, straddling his lap. His hands found their way under my skirt to grasp my ass, his finger tucking into the bottom edges of my panties.

"So, we're moving on to the *presents* part of the evening, are we?" he sassed, his eyes lighting up with that cocky charm that bowled me over—almost literally—from the first day we met.

"Who needs a list, anyway?" I said before slamming my mouth on his.

This kiss was nothing like the one we shared at the door. This one was full of the passion and heat we had kept pent up over the past few weeks. Hayden groaned into my mouth, his fingers flexing to grasp more of my ass, his fingers sliding under the fabric covering it and toward my center. One finger trailed down the seam of my ass, circling around the puckered hole briefly, causing my hips to thrust up.

Hayden pulled back to give me a questioning look.

"I mean, I'm not *not* into it. But I have other things in mind for tonight."

"Noted," Hayden said before moving his lips to my ear, then kissing down my neck and appreciating the neckline of my dress that scooped toward my cleavage. I buried my fingers in his hair, the silky texture grounding me in this place and time.

"Big fan of this dress," he murmured, pulling one hand out from under my skirt to pull the neckline down, causing a braless tit to pop out. "Big, big fan," he said, his eyes widening before tilting his head down to take my nipple in his mouth. I ground my hips into his lap, seeking the hand that lingered near my center, wanting more contact, more pressure, more something.

"I'd love to make you work for it, but maybe that's how we'll kick off the new year," Hayden said, pulling my neckline down further to reveal my other breast, repeating the treatment on the other side. "Right now, I'd just really like to be inside of you."

"Sounds like a plan to me," I said, reaching down to the hem of my dress and pulling it off in one swift motion, wincing when the firm texture of the hem of my neckline rubbed over my hardened nipples, as the fabric freed itself from where Hayden had left it under my boobs.

"Sensitive?" he asked, both his hands now running up and down my body, tickling my sides and cupping my breasts.

"Like that wasn't the plan. Too many clothes, Brandt."

"Too little room for movement, Reid."

I pushed my weight onto my knees, working at the button and zipper on his pants, while he got his sweater and undershirt up and over his head.

"Shoes and sock, Char."

I growled, impatient at the obstacles slowing me down. I maneuvered myself backward, freeing his cock from his open pants, untying his laces while licking stripes up and down the stiff rod that popped out to greet me.

And they say you can't truly multi-task, I thought, as I finished undoing the laces, needing my hands to help still Hayden's cock, as my mouth bobbed up and down.

Hayden's breaths came faster, and he yanked my hair, pulling me not-so-gently up and off the body part I was reacquainting myself with.

"That's on me. I should have been more specific, but I'd rather finish inside your pussy, if that works with your plans."

"All right, all right, if you must," I said, winking to soften the blow. The sex seemed to only get hotter, but the joking remained the same. I stood up, shimmying my panties down my legs as Hayden toed off his shoes and lifted his hips to pull his pants and briefs down.

His pants were around his ankles when my panties hit the ground, and he looked up and froze, gazing at me.

"What?" I said, gazing down at him.

"It's just... the glow of the tree, the city lights, you being you. You're gorgeous, Char, and I can't believe you're mine."

I lowered myself back onto this lap, knocking him back into gear to kick his pants the rest of the way off.

"Right back at ya, Hay," I said softly, running my hand down his face. He turned his lips into my palm, placing the softest of kisses there, holding it for a moment with his eyes closed. His eyes locked back on mine, and I reached down to grab his cock once more, this time holding it so I could hover over it and lower myself down slowly.

Hayden's hands grasped my hips, helping with the descent, and inch by inch, he slid back home. The stretch from this deep angle after a few weeks apart burned slightly, but Hayden moved his thumb to my clit, helping to relax my muscles and fully seat myself, my pelvis meeting his.

Hayden sucked in a breath, his eyes closed. "Fuck, I thought I had remembered how good you felt, all those nights with just my hand and your dirty texts, but I was wrong. This is better."

I started to move up slowly, riding the full length of him until he was almost fully removed from my center. The grip on my hips tightened, Hayden's teeth clenched, gritting out, "This isn't going to be long."

I leaned down to place a kiss on his shoulder before moving back and finding his eyes open, locking my gaze on his. "We have the rest of this year, and the next, and the next, and the next, and beyond, I hope."

Hayden nodded. "I hope so too."

"Then fuck me how you need me now, and get me there with you," I issued the challenge, Hayden's mouth dropping open.

"Sweet and sexy from one breath to the next. I'm a lucky guy," Hayden said as his hips pistoned up, filling me again and causing my head to fall back.

We fell into a quick rhythm together, his thumb moving on my clit in time with his thrusts. From this angle, I felt extra full, and his cock hit that spot deep inside me. Now I was the one who wouldn't last long.

"Fuck, fuck, fuck," Hayden said in time with his thrusts.

"Let go, Hay." He thrust up into me one more time and I felt the warmth of his release, his thumb still working at a firm and fast pace. The combination set me off the next moment, my walls clenching around his cock, extending his orgasm until I felt like I actually understood what romance novels meant when they said, "milked dry."

I rested my head on Hayden's shoulder as his arms wrapped around my back, one hand skating up and down from my shoulder blades to my lower back, as we returned to normal breathing together.

Hayden turned his head and kissed my hair. I let out a sigh of contentment, knowing we couldn't stay like this forever, but maybe for a few minutes longer. I thought about everything the past year had given me: the ups and the downs, the new career opportunities, the chance to find and fall in love with the man wrapped around me. I almost didn't know what to wish for in the new year.

"Whatcha thinking about, Char?"

"Just reflecting on the year. Do you make New Year's resolutions?" I lifted my head to meet his eyes.

Hayden shook his head. "I was afraid to want something, to

reach for something, until you showed me I was allowed. And I'm not sure how any new year could top this one."

I smiled. "That's my New Year's resolution then. To make sure it's filled with moments that make you look back and say, 'This is even better than I thought it could be.' I'm not going to promise all highs and no lows, but as long as there's at least one of those moments in a year, I think we'll be doing pretty good."

Hayden leaned in to kiss me. "I think we'll be doing even better than good. And maybe not this year, but I think my resolution one year will be to buy you a diamond you will wear every day. Just not around your neck."

A huge smile broke out across my face. "Maybe not this year. We should probably make it a whole year *choosing* to live together first. But I think someday, I'd be happy to wear your diamond daily."

"Happy New Year's," Hayden said, his eyes shining with happiness.

"Happy New Year's," I said back, perfectly aware mine were shining with a combination of happiness and tears.

Hayden shifted, settling himself against the couch from our place on the floor, arranging my back to his front. He pulled a blanket and wrapped it around us, not interested in separating our skin-on-skin contact. He reached to the side and grabbed the jewelry box from where I had left it on the ottoman, removing the necklace. I lifted my hair off my neck as he undid the clasp and laid the necklace against my skin, securing it in place.

My fingers reached up to finger the charm. "It's perfect."

We sat in silence for a few moments, enjoying the tree lights, the ambient city noise, and each other.

"Can you reach the remote?" I asked, breaking the silence and the moment.

"Really?" he said.

"We can put it on mute, but we have to watch Times Square.

Don't tell me you hate Ryan Seacrest," I said, my tone challenging him to disagree.

He laughed, reaching back to pull the remote off the arm of the couch.

"I wouldn't dare."

He turned the television on and surfed to the right channel as I nestled back into his body, a content smile on my face. I had no doubt we'd be happy, but we'd also never be bored. What a perfect match.

It's absolutely surreal that I'm sitting down to write my acknowledgements for my second book. Will the fear of leaving someone out ever lessen? Gosh, I hope so...

Lacey, thank you for your endless patience, understanding, cheerleading, and above all, excellent (as always) guidance during this book. Cassie, thank you for rolling with me and catching things at the umpteenth hour. Both of you, plus Ashley, Amber, Bethany and Chelsea, thank you for all the support, reality checks, safe space, help, and thirst trap Tik Toks on the daily.

Allie and Holly, supporting this project falls outside your assigned MFA critique group scope, yet you pulled me through this past year. I'm so grateful.

Izzy, Darrah, and Allie, I would be lost without you. You help me see through the imposter syndrome and believe in myself. Kelly, you're always ready to cheer me on or yell at someone, whatever I need. Steph, thanks for promising to never get sick of me. I promise to test that every chance I can. Emm, thanks for lending your name, I knew it looked just right when I typed it. The rest of Joyful Chaos, I never could have imagined this supportive group of friends who want me to succeed and celebrate every joyburst along with me like was their own. Thanks for proving my parents wrong about people you meet on the internet.

Dad, thanks for expanding beyond your normal non-fiction reads to read my books—outside the paper-clipped pages, please and thank you—and for learning a whole new set of vocabulary and industry terms to keep up with my day-to-day.

To my Allegheny girls and my DC friends, thanks for keeping me around even with all the talk about acronyms you don't understand, knotting, and dragon double eggplant emojis.

Jackie and Katie, thanks for helping me not always be that loner in Panera.

To all my ARC Readers, thank you for all you did to get the word out about this book; you helped readers know there was something worth picking up underneath this beautiful cover.

And to Dan, thanks for allowing my job to be (mostly) books. Betting on myself is a lot easier when you bet on me, too.

About the Author

Rachel grew up in Western PA and found her love of reading early in life, supported by her parents with frequent trips to the library and local bookstores. She stumbled into the online bookish world in late 2020 diving headfirst into the Romance genre. In 2021, she changed careers and took a job at a bookstore and started her first official novel-length writing project.

Now Rachel is getting an MFA in Popular Fiction at Seton Hill University and juggling too many story ideas for one brain to handle. She's excited to continue to share Happily Ever Afters with you that bring the laughs and the love.

When not immersed in her bookish world, you can find Rachel hanging out with her husband and two cats, spending time with friends in the Washington DC area, and rooting for Pittsburgh sports teams.

Also by Rachel Holm

HOLLY RIDGE SERIES

Carry Me Through Christmas
Coming Soon: Make You Mine This Christmas

THE BRANDT BROTHERS SERIES

Capitally Matched

Capitally Engaged

Capitally Unexpected

Coming Soon: Capitally Yours